Alex's voice became aggressive

"If you say another damn word to anyone about my family in England," he said, "I'll make sure you're railroaded out of this town in the morning."

As Alex finished his speech, the band struck up again, and for a moment Laura didn't take in the full meaning of his statement. Then she realized how far her optimistic hopes were from being achieved, and instinctively pulled away from him.

His hands promptly hauled her back.

"Maybe you reckon it makes no difference to me what you say about them," he went on in the same low but firm voice, "but I'm telling you, it does."

Laura took a couple of deep breaths, hiding her angry disappointment, and found her tongue. "But why? Why? They're nothing to be ashamed of."

SALLY COOK lives in Norwich with her two small sons. She was a professional writer for nine years before she branched into romance fiction.

Books by Sally Cook

Don't miss any of our special offers. Write to us at the following address for information on our newest releases.

Harlequin Reader Service
P.O. Box 1397, Buffalo, NY 14240
Canadian address: P.O. Box 603,
Fort Erie, Ont. L2A 5X3

SALLY COOK

inherit your love

Harlequin Books

TORONTO • NEW YORK • LONDON
AMSTERDAM • PARIS • SYDNEY • HAMBURG
STOCKHOLM • ATHENS • TOKYO • MILAN

Harlequin Presents first edition March 1992
ISBN 0-373-11440-0

Original hardcover edition published in 1990
by Mills & Boon Limited

INHERIT YOUR LOVE

CHAPTER ONE

'WHAT a maddening man!'

Laura Mallingham looked up in surprise. Lady Exonby was normally soft-voiced, but this time she had spoken with something close to fury.

'Who?'

'Alex. Alex Gillon. He's written me an absolutely infuriating letter.'

Who *was* Alex Gillon? Laura wondered. Lady Exonby had spoken as if she would know, but she didn't. Gillon was the Exonbys' family name, though, so he had to be a relation. 'Oh, dear,' she said, hoping this would produce some more information.

It did. 'And after taking an absolute age to reply,' Lady Exonby went on. 'As usual. I told him it was urgent, too. Heavens, I must have last written in——' She pulled out one of her desk drawers, reached in for a slim buff folder, and checked the contents before continuing, 'January. The twenty-seventh.'

'That's nearly four months ago.' It was also a month before Laura had started work at Exonby Hall, so it was no wonder she hadn't a clue what the infuriating letter was about.

'Indeed. And now to write to me in this tone . . . You read it, dear, and tell me that I'm not being over-sensitive.'

'I'm sure you're not, Lady Exonby,' Laura murmured, rising from her table in the corner and crossing to where Lady Exonby sat at the desk. The study at Exonby Hall was a large room, oak-panelled, and the scent of wallflowers came through the half-opened windows that gave on to the front terrace.

The letter Lady Exonby handed over so disdainfully turned out to be a single thick sheet of paper, with a big bold-printed heading. This had a little picture of a car sitting on a platter balanced on the palm of a large hand, drawn in a bold cartoon style. To its right was the fat black word 'Northways', with a smaller caption underneath: 'We serve up the best Fords in New Mexico'.

'New Mexico?'

'The man's clearly never heard of airmail paper. He never normally writes personal letters either, from the look of it.'

True, it didn't look like a personal letter, even if you overlooked the letterhead. The single paragraph was neatly typed—word processed, rather, Laura decided, taking in the even margins—and laid out business fashion. The signature was large and scrawling, barely legible. She read:

> 'Dear Lady Exonby,
> Thank you for your letter. As I have told you before, I do not want to return to England. I am now settled in the US, and plan to remain here for the rest of my life. I am sure you and Lord Exonby are running the estate just fine, and you have my word that I will not cause you any hassle in the future. Do whatever you think fit with the place.
>
> > Yours truly,
> > A G Gillon.'

'Well?' Lady Exonby demanded.

Laura frowned. It wasn't the kind of personal letter Lady Exonby normally received, but it wasn't deliberately rude or provocative—was it?

'It seems very clear,' she said tentatively.

'Oh, it's clear,' Lady Exonby retorted, 'but it's not acceptable.'

'I'm not sure I understand, Lady Exonby. Is Mr Gillon a relation of his lordship's?'

'Not just a relation, *the* relation. George's nephew. His father Sandy died four or five years ago, so this young man——' Lady Exonby stabbed a neatly manicured forefinger at the sheet of paper '—is now the heir to the earldom.'

'I see,' Laura said. Her eyes came back to the letter. It could hardly have been more different from the letters Lord and Lady Exonby wrote, by hand, on notepaper half this size topped with a discreet coronet. No flowery phrases, no enquiries about their health, no family chit-chat at all!

'You can see it won't do.'

Obviously not, Laura thought with a shudder of distaste. A brash garageman from New Mexico as the Fourth Earl of Exonby? How appalling!

But Lady Exonby wasn't objecting to Mr Gillon himself, she realised, so much as to his refusal to come back to England. He *was* the heir to the earldom, and she wanted him welcomed into his rightful place quickly, since the present Lord Exonby could hardly live more than a very few months longer.

Laura appreciated all this instinctively. Her own father was an earl too, though the Mallinghams didn't possess a huge and historic country estate like the Exonbys. Now she could see how every nuance in Alex Gillon's letter would have rubbed Lady Exonby up the wrong way. Obviously Lady Exonby had set about the distasteful business of bringing this uncouth American back to Exonby with all her usual brisk determination. No wonder this blunt refusal had left her—by her sedate standards—hopping mad.

'What a very difficult situation,' Laura said gently.

'Very.'

'Do you know Mr Gillon personally, your ladyship?'

'I knew him when he was a boy. Not intimately. George and Sandy never hit it off too well, and Sandy's wife—well, frankly, my dear, that was a disaster. But we always had them to stay here twice a year, and, since it was clear from the start that young Alex would be the heir, George did everything he could to interest the boy in the estate.'

'I'm sure any boy would be thrilled to realise that all this would one day be his.'

'Not young Alex. He was always a thorough——' Lady Exonby leaned forward, as if she was about to go into a lengthy catalogue of Alex Gillon's sins, then she seemed to remember that Laura was not one of the family, drew back swiftly, and said in a different tone of voice, 'He was a very lively young boy.'

'But he must be considerably older now?'

'Let's see. He was eighteen or nineteen when he emigrated, and that was . . . pass me that copy of *Debrett's*, my dear.'

Laura reached for the fat red volume, and watched Lady Exonby leaf through the pages.

'Here we are. "Exonby, Earl of . . . Nephew living. Alexander George, born 1953." So he's in his late thirties now.'

'His late thirties? Then Alexander senior must have been in his fifties when Alex junior was born?'

'I suppose he was. He wasn't a marrying man, Sandy. He stayed a bachelor till he was fifty or so. His wife was much younger, of course. There's a daughter too, a couple of years younger than Alex.'

'Did she emigrate as well?'

'Oh, no. Married a shopkeeper or somebody.'

Lady Exonby's voice was dismissive. She shut *Debrett's* with a resounding thud. Laura was tempted to reach for it and peep at the entry, but she decided that would be tactless.

'So you haven't met Mr Gillon since the early seventies, your ladyship?'

'Not once. He never wrote even to his own mother. He might have disappeared off the face of the earth. A couple of years ago George had Jeremy Flowerdew track down an address for him, and since then we've written a dozen times, but never had more than a paragraph in reply.' She glanced disparagingly at the thin folder, then picked it up and handed it over to Laura.

Laura leafed through it, a little self-consciously. Most of her work for Lady Exonby had been less personal than this, and, though she was being invited to look, she still felt uneasy about reading private letters. But there was nothing interesting in them, as she soon discovered. A sheaf of lengthy letters from Lord and Lady Exonby and from Jeremy Flowerdew, their solicitor, were interleaved with the occasional one-paragraph reply from Alex Gillon, all of them typed, all on the 'Northways' letterhead, all revealing nothing except the fact that Mr Gillon did not intend to come back to England.

When she reached the end she set the folder back down on Lady Exonby's desk.

'What am I to do?' Lady Exonby asked distractedly.

'Perhaps it would be best not to do anything, your ladyship. It doesn't sound as if Mr Gillon would have very much in common with his lordship, and if he were to come over it might be a little uncomfortable for everyone. Perhaps in a few months you'll want to write again, and——'

'After George dies?' Lady Exonby interrupted her.

'Well...'

'Don't be squeamish, girl. We both know perfectly well he's on the way out. And he's ninety-two, for heaven's sake, so he's had a very good innings. But that won't do, my dear. Think of the tenants. We must plan the transition properly.'

'But if Mr Gillon is adamant that he doesn't want to come and live on the estate——'

'He must,' Lady Exonby said sharply. 'The Gillons of Exonby have lived here for over four hundred years. He absolutely must.'

There was a pile of other correspondence to be seen to, a steady stream of phone calls and a few visitors coming to the Hall, and Laura soon forgot about Alex Gillon's letter. She worked with Lady Exonby till lunch, then after lunch her employer set out as usual on visits to elderly tenants before returning to take tea with her bedridden husband. Laura worked on alone.

She was typing out a letter to the secretary of the local pony club when Mason, the butler, knocked on the door.

'You're wanted upstairs, Lady Laura. By his lordship.'

She jumped to her feet. 'There's not anything...?'

'They're having tea, miss.'

'I'll go right away.'

She switched off her ancient electric typewriter and made her way down the long corridors of Exonby Hall towards the main staircase. The house had been built in the late eighteenth century, and she knew it was far too large by modern standards, but it had a sedate charm to it, and she could understand why Lord and Lady Exonby loved the place so much.

Up the main staircase, past a marble bust of the first earl on one landing and one of the second countess in the next, and she was nearly at the earl's private rooms. She knocked gently, and Lady Exonby's voice called out to her to come in.

The room was a little stuffy on the warm spring day, though one of the windows was slightly open. The big bed, piled high with bolsters, dominated the room, but

Lord Exonby was up for once, sitting opposite his wife in an easy chair by the fireplace.

'Do bring up a chair, Laura,' Lady Exonby said.

Laura sat. Lady Exonby was already pouring the tea, the usual Earl Grey, into china cups so thin they were almost transparent. A plate of cheese and egg sandwiches and another of sliced Madeira cake sat on the low table.

'So Florry has told you about my rogue of a nephew,' Lord Exonby said.

'George,' Lady Exonby scolded, 'we've no reason to think he's a rogue.'

'Rubbish. You can see from the notepaper the man's a garage mechanic. No wonder, he always was as thick as two short planks. Always had his nose under a car bonnet, too. But he's Sandy's son all the same, and he's got to fill his place. The estate's entailed, so I've no choice but to pass it on to him. I don't want there to be any trouble when I pop off. I'm not having some accursed Texan throwing the tenants out of work or harassing Florry when she moves into the Dower House, so we've got to bring him over now and remind him how things are done over here.'

'I quite understand, your lordship. But—well, I've read the file, and it seems to me that everything that can be done has already been done.'

'Not everything.'

'Would you like me to write to Mr Flowerdew? I could ask him to——'

Lord Exonby shook his head. 'What I'd like, my dear, is for you to go to New Mexico and haul young Alex back with you.'

'Me!'

'Don't you see, Laura?' Lady Exonby said eagerly. 'You're the perfect person. We can't ask Jeremy Flowerdew to go—he'd charge a fortune!—but somebody simply must go and make Alex see sense. It's an ideal job for a woman. Alex may be a little rough-edged, but he *is* a Gillon, and he had a public school education, so he'd never be anything but a perfect gentleman towards a lady. If you ask him to come back to England with you, I can't see how he can possibly refuse!'

I can! Laura thought to herself. Go to New Mexico, hunt out a complete stranger and ask him to do something he's been flatly refusing to do for the past two years—it sounded totally unsuitable. More than that, it sounded impossible!

'Really, Lady Exonby, I don't think——'

'No, don't think,' Lord Exonby broke in, with unexpected strength. 'Don't think of all the reasons why not, my dear. Think of it as a great adventure. You'll be doing it as a favour to me and Florry, but we want you to make a real holiday of it, and enjoy yourself while you're over there. We've friends in New York who would put you up for a few days, and in South Carolina too. You'll have a wonderful time.'

'But I'm not sure that I could do it! What if Mr Gillon won't talk to me? What if he isn't prepared to——?'

'Then you'll have to come back and tell us so,' Lady Exonby said. 'We won't expect miracles, my dear. But you're a clever young lady, and a charming one.' Her eyes seemed to check Laura out, taking in the long blonde hair, neatly fastened away in a pony-tail, the regular features, the sensible but attractive cream blouse and beige slub silk skirt, the three-stranded pearl choker that she had inherited from her grandmother and always wore, and seemed to confirm that all of this ought to act as a good advertisement. 'You're the best ambassadress for Exonby and all it stands for that we could possibly have.'

'But what would Anthony say?'

'Oh, bother Anthony!' Lord Exonby retorted. 'You're not married to him yet, Laura. You make the best of your freedom while you still have it.'

After dinner that evening Laura retreated to her own room, high in the west wing of the hall, and picked up the telephone.

She still wasn't sure if she should agree to go, though she had promised to think it over. Perhaps her parents would tell her that it was a ridiculous idea?

They didn't; they were delighted. It would be a wonderful and exciting opportunity to see something of the States, they both agreed, and there was much to be said, too, for getting to know the future Earl of Exonby. Laura rang off twenty minutes later with a long list of names and phone numbers of relations and acquaintances in the States, and a promise from her mother to write with still more.

That's it, she thought in amazement. I really am going to New Mexico.

She sat there for a moment, lost in thought, then picked up the phone again to dial another familiar number.

'Lady Downing? It's Laura. Could I speak to Anthony, please?'

'He's in the gun-room, I think, dear. I'll just go and fetch him.'

Laura smiled to herself as she pictured Anthony cleaning his beloved collection of rifles. There was a minute's silence, then his familiar deep voice came on to the line.

'Laura? This isn't the usual time for you to ring.'

'I know, but I've some exciting news. Could I come over—this evening, or tomorrow?'

'I'm having the vicar round to sherry this evening. Come to supper tomorrow—about six-thirty?'

'I'll see you then.'

'Gillon? *Alex Gillon?*'

'That's right, Anthony. He's Lord Exonby's heir. Why, do you know him?'

'I used to know an Alex Gillon. I suppose it must be the same chap. We were at Darlingforth together. He was a year or two younger than me, a real—well, never mind that. Gosh, I never—but come to think, he must be old Exonby's nephew or something.'

'Nephew exactly,' Laura confirmed. She and Anthony were walking together, after supper, in the High Wood at Maltwood House, Anthony's home. Anthony, like her, was wearing green wellingtons and a snug drab-olive parka. He looked precisely what he was, a successful farmer with business interests in the city. He was a handsome man in a rather thickset way, with crisply waving brown hair brushed off his forehead, and a short, bristly moustache. Just the sort of man one married, as Laura had told herself on Christmas Eve, when she had received—and accepted—the proposal she had been expecting for some time.

Her glance told her he was frowning.

'A real what, Anthony?'

'Oh, you've probably heard it all already. A drop-out, a tearaway. A no good. Real duffer, Gillon was—the type who couldn't add two and two. Not that he ever tried, as I recall. I never knew a boy with such a knack for dodging lessons. In his last year he set an all-time record for the number of canings. They said he'd have been expelled if he hadn't been so handy on the rugby field.'

'He was good at games?'

'Ace. An absolute whizz. Run, jump, throw—Gillon could do it all. But put a pen in his hand and he fell to pieces.' Anthony stalked on for a few more paces, seemingly lost in memories, then he came to an abrupt halt. 'Darling,' he said, 'I don't think you should go.'

'My first thought was to refuse, Anthony,' Laura said quietly. 'But I've thought it over, and I feel I should go. It's part of my job, and the Exonbys have been very good to me. It's the least I can do for them in return.'

'But you don't understand. You don't know him; you don't know what you'll be getting into.'

Laura felt a touch of her original uncertainty return, then, almost to her own surprise, a little surge of annoyance flooded it out. She wasn't usually adventurous, but she had warmed to the idea of making this bizarre American trip before she settled down to married life at Maltwood. She wasn't going to let Anthony talk her out of it!

'That's true. But you don't know him either, Anthony. It's nearly twenty years since you last met Alex Gillon.'

'Yes, but the things he did then! What he was like then...'

'Anthony, it's true Alex Gillon doesn't sound like somebody I'd want to ask to dinner, but that's no reason for me to refuse to go and speak to him.'

'Darling, he's dangerous!' A flush came over Anthony's ruddy cheeks. 'I know it sounds silly, but—well, I'm afraid of what he might do to you. You're not used to dealing with unprincipled wolves, and a nice girl like you, alone in a strange country—Exonby should have realised at once that it's just not on!'

'Not on? But, Anthony, this is the end of the twentieth century! I'm not planning to cross the Sahara single-handed! I've been to Paris alone, and Venice, and I'm told the natives are quite friendly in New Mexico!'

'I don't want you dealing with Gillon,' Anthony said stubbornly.

'Anthony darling.' Laura did her best to hide her growing exasperation, as she moved towards her fiancé and slipped her arm under his elbow. 'You surely know,' she went on, 'that I'm not interested in that kind of man. You can't imagine I'm that kind of girl!'

'I know you're not,' Anthony said awkwardly. 'But I still don't want you to go, Laura.'

'Well, I'm sorry, darling, but I'm afraid that now I have to go.'

They walked on in silence for a couple of minutes. Laura half expected Anthony to make another attempt to dissuade her, but he didn't say anything more. He wasn't a forceful man. Steady, competent, he always moved slowly and cautiously. It was his earlier vehemence that had been out of character, and for him to positively demand that she not go to New Mexico would be even more out of character. In fact, Laura thought to herself, there could hardly be more of a contrast between two people than between the Anthony she knew and the Alex Gillon he had just described. Alex Gillon might blunder through life like a charging rhino, but Anthony's own approach was much more temperate.

Boring, Lady Exonby had once suggested in an odd flash of temper. Laura had laughed off the insult then, but now it suddenly came back to her. No strange woman would feel threatened in hunting out Sir Anthony Downing! He certainly wouldn't make a pass at them; indeed, he had never made a pass at Laura.

But didn't she like that? Didn't it please her to know that Anthony's temperament was as cool as her own, and that he was happy to wait until their marriage, without rushing into messy and undignified fumbles beforehand? Of course she liked it, she told herself firmly, as Anthony slowly circled around and began to walk with her back towards Maltwood House.

CHAPTER TWO

LAURA stepped out of Albuquerque airport and into a wall of hot air. It was like walking through a sauna bath. She found it difficult to move, difficult even to think. Fortunately her hire car was parked only a few yards away, and soon she was subsiding on to a scalding seat, slipping the key into the ignition, and switching on the air-conditioning.

She cast her eye over the unfamiliar controls. It was a Ford, an automatic. Then something snagged on the edge of her mind, and she glanced back and realised what it was. Stuck at the edge of the windscreen was a little logo of a car on a platter, drawn in cartoon style. Underneath the hand which held it up was the single word 'Northways'.

Northways? That was the name—and the logo—of Alex Gillon's garage, but the small town where he worked was over a hundred and fifty miles from Albuquerque. Curious, she glanced quickly through the car particulars. Sure enough it had been supplied by Northways, though the address given was not the one written in her pocket-book, but one in Albuquerque itself.

So much, she thought, for the Exonbys' theory that Alex Gillon runs a small garage of his own. Obviously he works for a large chain. Is he a mechanic, I wonder, or could he be the manager of the local branch?

If only she had a private address for him! She had contacted his mother and sister before leaving England, but their only response had been brief notes saying that they knew nothing at all about his present life, so all she had to go on was the address of the Northways branch.

She felt weary, hot and sweaty. Starting the car, she swung out on to the freeway to downtown Albuquerque and her hotel. She deserved a good rest: the remainder of the journey could wait a day.

Next morning she drove east, through a bleakly dramatic landscape of mountains, cactus plants and rough scrubland. By lunchtime she was over the Manzano Mountains, and moving down the gentler landscape of the Pecos river valley towards Carlsbad and the border with Texas. Finally a signpost announced her destination, and almost immediately beyond it was the entrance to the motel where she had booked a room.

The Marbury Motel was luxurious. It had a restaurant and coffee shop, a swimming-pool that looked invitingly cold and blue, and long, cool corridors.

Laura almost threw off the white trousers and T-shirt she had worn for the drive, and switched on the shower as soon as the porter had left the room. She lingered under the jets for a quarter of an hour, and washed the grime out of her hair too before pinning it back in a neat chignon and slipping on a sleeveless pink cotton sun-dress.

How funny, she thought, peeping at her reflection in the full-length mirror. It was the same Laura that she always saw—the same long, straight fair hair, the same pale skin, the same kind of simple, understated dress, the same strands of pearls. Nothing had changed, but somehow she looked different—foreign, as if the face and clothes that she had thought wouldn't attract notice anywhere simply didn't fit into this place.

In every way she was totally different from the women she had seen since getting off the plane. Her lack of a suntan, her minimal make-up, her air of diffidence, all seemed un-American. All the Americans she had talked to had exclaimed on her darling accent, too—while she had found it hard to decipher a word they said!

She felt conspicuous, an unfamiliar and uncomfortable feeling for her. But there wasn't anything she could do about it—she didn't know how to look or act like an American.

At least everybody had been friendly, greeting her with lively enthusiasm, so perhaps, she thought, Alex Gillon would turn out to be the same. But first she had to find him. She began her search by checking the local telephone directory, but maddeningly it turned out to have no 'Gillon, A's listed. Then she checked with the telephone operator, but soon learned that she couldn't provide a number for Alex Gillon either.

It would have to be the garage. She went downstairs, and the motel receptionist showed her how to get there on a town plan. 'Park on Main,' she said. 'Then it's two blocks west, see. The avenues go this way and the streets that, so here's the junction of Fifteenth Street and Third Avenue.'

'How very logical.'

'You can't get lost there,' the girl said with a smile. 'Have a nice day.'

It was already late afternoon, but Laura felt she ought to make a start on finding—and persuading—Alex Gillon as soon as possible. She drove downtown. To her surprise the junction of Main and Fifteenth turned out to be right in the centre of the downtown shopping area. She parked and walked up to Third Avenue. The pavements were lined with offices all the way.

310, Fifteenth Street, the address she had written down, wasn't a repair shop or a car showroom; it was another office block, bigger and taller than most, with huge glass doors leading into an atrium where a forest of greenery clustered around a fountain. She paused outside and looked up and down the streets. She couldn't be lost. So what had happened to Northways Garage?

The office block entrance was down a couple of steps. Oh, come on, Laura, she told herself. You haven't come all this way just to give up at the first hurdle. Be pushy and forthright and more like the people here! Go and ask!

She went down the steps and peered at the doors. On each one was inscribed the familiar Northways logo. So this really was it—but 'it' wasn't a small local branch of the Northways chain. This, surely, was the head office.

Inside, the block was so heavily air-conditioned that it was almost cold. Behind the fountain was a long reception desk.

'Can I help you, honey?' drawled the receptionist.

'I hope so, yes.'

'Hey, your *accent*! Don't tell me—you're from Boston?'

Laura couldn't help smiling at this misplaced confidence. 'Not even close. I'm from England.'

'England! Wow! So what you doing in New Mexico?'

'Actually, I've come to meet another English person. A Mr Gillon, who works here?'

'Mr Gillon?'

'His first name's Alex—Alex Gillon?'

'Sure Alex Gillon works here, honey, but he's about as English as I am!'

'He's been in the States for a long time.'

'All his life, I'd swear. Alex Gillon's a Yankee through and through.'

Not quite, Laura thought. But she didn't want to start arguing about Alex Gillon's background, so she just said, 'Is Mr Gillon in? Would it be possible to have a word with him?'

'I think he's in, but he's a busy man. You made an appointment?'

'I'm afraid not. It's—it's a personal matter. If I can just have a quick word with him now, I hope I'll be able to arrange to meet up with him again. Outside office hours.'

The receptionist gave her a more appraising look, as if she was trying to judge whether Laura might be a girl-friend of some kind. She frowned slightly, then said coolly, 'So who shall I say's here?'

'Laura Mallingham—but he won't know the name, I'm afraid.'

'Just a moment, Miss Mallingham.'

She picked up her telephone, and was soon talking away in a loud whisper. Laura tried not to listen. How embarrassing all this was.

The receptionist put the phone down. 'Mr Gillon's pretty busy, Miss Mallingham, but you can go up and leave a message with his secretary if you'd care to.'

Leave a message? That wasn't the start she had been hoping for. But she sensed that this was all she would be offered, and she couldn't afford to refuse. Maybe his secretary—his *personal* secretary?—would be able to fill in some more background.

'I'll do that. Which way is it?'

'The end elevator goes express to the top floor.'

The top floor! Wouldn't that be the boss's office? Alex Gillon surely couldn't be *that* high up in an organisation as large as Northways!

Confused and disorientated, apprehensive about her whole mission, Laura made her way to the lift. A moment later she was stepping out into a second reception area. This one was carpeted in deep red, with many more plants, and a large square of desks out from which stepped a pretty, dark-haired woman.

'Hello there, Miss Mallingham. I'm Gloria.'

'Actually,' Laura said nervously, 'I'm not Miss Mallingham. I'm Lady Laura Mallingham.'

'An English lady! Oh, boy! I'm real pleased to meet you, Lady Mallingham.'

'It's Lady Laura, not Lady Mallingham. I'm sorry, I know English titles are confusing. My mother is called Lady Mallingham, while I'm Lady Laura Mallingham, or Lady Laura for short.' She felt that she was being idiotically fussy, but she knew Alex Gillon, who had grown up among the aristocracy, would remember these niceties, and she wanted to be introduced to him correctly.

'Let me write that down,' Gloria said good-naturedly. Laura followed her to the desk, and dictated the spelling to her. On the desk-top she could see a pile of newly typed letters. At the foot of each one was Alex Gillon's signature, just as she had seen it before. At least this is the same Alex Gillon, she thought. I haven't mistaken that.

'Mr Gillon's real busy, Lady Laura. Shannon didn't say what you wanted to see him about?'

'Actually it's a personal matter. I'm an associate of his relations in England. We've never met before, but I've brought a letter of introduction from Mr Gillon's uncle.' She reached in her handbag, and brought out the long crested vellum envelope.

Gloria took the letter, turned it over, then said, 'I'll take it in to him.'

Laura took the seat she was offered, watched Gloria disappear through a pair of mahogany doors at the far end of the reception area, and then glanced around her. On a low table the local newspapers and the *Washington Post* were spread out, together with a glossy annual report for Northways. She picked this up, and opened the cover. The first page confirmed what she already suspected: there, in black and white, A G Gillon was listed as president and chief executive of the Northways Group.

She flicked through the rest of the report. Northways was a private company, she saw, and Mr Gillon was the major shareholder. It had offices in three states, and a very large turnover. Alex Gillon was no simple garage hand. She wasn't an expert on financial statements, but she felt sure that he must be a millionaire many times over.

So the notorious school dunce that Anthony remembered had made good in a big way! No wonder he wasn't wildly excited at the thought of inheriting Exonby, she thought. He must already possess all the material wealth he could use—and more.

A moment later Gloria reappeared. 'Mr Gillon says to thank you, Lady Laura.'

'Will he see me now?' Laura asked, rising to her feet.

'Why, he didn't say anything, Lady Laura. I gave him the letter. Wasn't that what you came for?'

No, it wasn't, not at all. She summoned up all her confidence, and went on with quiet persistence, 'The letter was by way of an introduction, to explain to him who I was. I came to see him in person, not just to hand it over.'

'Then I'm sorry, Lady Laura. He must have misunderstood.'

'That's all right. Is he free now? Could I have a brief word with him?'

'I'm afraid not.'

'Then could I make an appointment, please? To see him tomorrow, or later in the week?'

'Mr Gillon didn't suggest that, Lady Laura.'

'Then I'm suggesting it.'

'I can't make an appointment for you without Mr Gillon's approval, I'm afraid.'

A cold shiver went down Laura's spine. She couldn't fail now. Not yet. She couldn't go home without at least talking to Alex Gillon.

'Then please go back and get it,' she said with an un-familiar surge of determination.

'I'm real sorry, Lady Laura, but I can't do that. Mr Gillon's already left, you see.'

'Rubbish!'

Gloria was either a good actress, or she was used to scenes like this, because she didn't quail at all. 'I'm sorry,' she repeated in a cool voice.

'Look,' Laura said, 'you don't understand. I've come all the way from England to see Mr Gillon.'

'I'm real sorry, Lady Laura.'

'Are you hell!'

Laura's patience snapped, finally and completely. She couldn't give up now! It wouldn't be right, wouldn't be fair, not when she'd come so far! Alex Gillon simply had to see her!

And, curse him, he would! She darted past the other woman, round the end of the square of desks, and to-wards the double doors that evidently led to Mr Gillon's office. 'Lady Laura!' Gloria shouted from behind her. But it was too late. Laura had already reached the doors, and flung them open.

There, confronting her, was a large and completely empty office. Executive desk, easy chairs, low tables, loaded bookshelves, a computer—and not a trace of Mr Gillon.

'You see, Lady Laura,' Gloria said at her elbow, 'he really has gone. Normally he works on till six at least, but there's a charity ball tonight at the Marbury Motel, and he left early to get ready for that. He's on the com-mittee, you see.'

'But he didn't pass us. I was out there the whole time, and he——'

'There's a private elevator over in the corner,' Gloria said gently, pointing to a discreet padded door that Laura hadn't noticed.

*   *   *

Fifteen minutes later Laura was back sitting on the bed in her motel room, sipping a Diet Coke from the fridge, and wondering what to do next.

It really had been unforgivable of her to snap at Gloria. The other woman had only been doing her job. But her jet lag, the heat, the surprise of learning that Alex Gillon wasn't the garage hand she had expected to meet—all of these things had conspired to weaken her self-control.

She had apologised afterwards, of course, and Gloria had been as pleasant as ever. But she had refused either to make Laura an appointment, or to give out Alex Gillon's private address and telephone number.

Still, Laura knew one thing now. He would be at the Marbury Motel that evening for the charity ball. So she would just have to find him there.

She went for a quick dip in the pool to revive her flagging spirits, then she returned to the motel reception and asked for the manager. She introduced herself by her full title, and asked if there was any chance that she might drop in on the charity ball that evening.

'*Lady* Laura, you say?'

'That's right,' Laura agreed, with her brightest, most aristocratic smile.

'Hey, do you know the Queen? And Princess Di?'

'Both of them,' Laura assured him. In fact she had met them only briefly, but she didn't tell the manager that.

'I'm sure they'd be honoured to have you there, your ladyship. Mind, you'd have to speak to Susie-Jo Allen—she's the chairwoman of the ball committee.'

'Could I do that now?'

'I'll call her right away.'

Five minutes later it was fixed. Mrs Allen had assured Laura that she would be thrilled to meet her, and to invite her to the ball as a special guest of the committee. Laura had promised to come down early to meet the Allens before the rest of the guests arrived, and she had agreed to tell Mrs Allen everything she knew about Princess Di.

In England, she would have cringed at pushing herself forward like this, let alone at making use of her title in such a blatant way. Mrs Allen hadn't come across as snobbish, though. She simply sounded thrilled at the prospect of meeting a real English lady who knew the Queen. Laura had said that she was in the States on vacation—which was, after all, partly true—and Mrs Allen had accepted that readily, assuming that she would have come to this part of New Mexico to see the Carlsbad Caverns.

The *what*? Laura wondered, wishing her quick preparations had taken in a guidebook or two. A trip back to the reception found her a shower of leaflets, though, and she soon felt that she knew enough about the local tourist attractions to get by.

She hadn't mentioned Alex Gillon's name once.

It took her all the short time that was left to get ready for the ball. Fortunately she had packed one long dress, a slinky, uncrushable length of blue polyester which proved to have survived the journey well. She twisted her damp hair back into a knot, slipped on pearl drop earrings to match her choker, and made her face up with extra care, applying blusher, two shades of blue eyeshadow and three coatings of mascara to make the most of her long, but naturally pale lashes.

Would that do? It certainly wasn't overdone, she realised, as the hotel manager introduced her to Susie-Jo Allen and her husband Kent. Mrs Allen was younger than she had expected, not more than thirty, but extremely glamorous, with perfectly coiffed streaked blonde hair, a dramatic backless red dress, and lashings of gold jewellery. A western-style band was already tuning up in the ballroom, and from the look of the tables there would be a lavish banquet before the dancing.

'You really picked the right time to come,' Mrs Allen assured her. 'This is the biggest evening of the year round here. I wish I'd known sooner, and I could have found you an escort. But you come and sit with us, and I'll swear every man in the room will want to dance with you.'

'I sure will,' Kent Allen agreed, with a lazy smile. He was a tall, thin man with a narrow-boned face, sharply dressed in a dinner-jacket with a western-style bootlace tie. 'It's a real treat to meet a foreigner. We don't get many round these parts.'

'Round here, somebody from Albuquerque's a foreigner,' his wife added with a smile.

'But you must have some first-generation immigrants from Europe, surely?'

'Can't think of any,' Kent Allen said firmly. 'Mexicans, yes, and a few Puerto Ricans, but we don't have any big immigrant communities. Mind you, Lady Laura, my family come from England way back. An Allen was Lord Mayor of London in the fourteenth century.'

'Really?'

'You come from London, I guess?'

'I'm afraid not. I live in Gloucestershire.'

'Don't mean a thing, honey.'

Laura spent the next ten minutes trying to explain where Gloucestershire was. Around them, the room was steadily filling. One or two people came over and greeted the Allens, and a waiter brought round a tray of cocktails. The Allens had to tell Laura what they were, and they found it hilarious that she had never had a Tequila Sunrise before. It was delicious, she assured them, sipping the cold, multi-coloured layers of drink.

She listened carefully as people were introduced to her, but she didn't hear the name Gillon. She glanced occasionally round the room, but none of the swaggering males and their glamorous wives reminded her of the Exonbys at all.

Susie-Jo dashed off to check on the band's arrangements, and Kent introduced Laura to the chairman of a local computer company, a short, plump man, and his dark, svelte wife.

'Hey, Kent, what've you done with Susie-Jo?'

The loud, harsh-toned voice at her shoulder made Laura swing round. It belonged to a tall man with tawny hair and a strong-featured, weather-beaten face.

'She's over by the band,' Kent said. 'Haven't swapped her, Alex, I'm just busy introducing our visitor to everyone.'

'So who's the beautiful lady?'

Alex. Was this him? Laura gave a polite but wary smile, and held out her hand. The compliment didn't impress her—a whole stream of American men, so different from the restrained English she was used to, had already assured her she was the most gorgeous thing they'd ever seen.

She met his eyes, and a jolt of sheer electricity went through her, rooting her to the floor. He had the strongest dose of animal magnetism she had ever encountered. He wasn't handsome, but he oozed power and authority. His light brown eyes held her so firmly that she simply couldn't look away.

'Would you believe, Alex, she's a real lady, come all the way from Gloucestershire, England. Lady Laura, this is Alex Gillon, head of Northways Garages. Alex, meet Lady Laura Mallingham.'

CHAPTER THREE

A FORK of lightning seemed to flash somewhere within Alex Gillon's light brown eyes.

'How the hell did you get in here?'

Laura flushed, dragged her glance away from him, and cast a nervous smile at Kent Allen.

'Hey,' said the computer boss, 'you two know each other?'

'Not exactly,' Laura managed to say. 'Back in England I work for Mr Gillon's——'

'We have some mutual acquaintances,' Alex Gillon cut in roughly.

Laura's eyes came back to him before she could stop herself. His brows were lowered now, and his eyes seemed to have darkened several shades.

'In England?' Kent Allen said incredulously.

'Alex, honey, what's all this?'

A short blonde girl with an exquisite, fairy face had appeared by Alex Gillon's side, and was pulling on his arm. 'Hey,' she went on, turning to Laura, 'you new round here? I don't recognise your face.'

'Let me do the introductions. Lady Laura Mallingham—Darlene Dixon,' Kent Allen said hastily. 'Lady Laura's fresh over from England, Darlene. And we've just learned that she and Alex——'

'I was over in England when I was a kid,' Alex said, cutting off Kent as firmly as he had interrupted Laura earlier. 'Lady Laura brought me a message from an old acquaintance. Which sure was kind of her, but all that's so far back in my life now that I barely remember it.'

Barely remember his own aunt and uncle! 'Maybe that's true,' Laura retorted, 'but your "acquaintances" certainly remember you, Mr Gillon.'

'You've lived in England, Alex?' Darlene Dixon cried. 'Oh, boy! Alex Gillon, I must've known you ten years, and I've never in all that time heard you mention living in England.'

'I don't think about it much.'

'So how long were you there for?' Kent Allen asked.

'When I was a kid. Years ago. I haven't been back for close on twenty years.'

He said this offhandedly, his face blank, his composure clearly regained. Laura herself, meanwhile, was feeling more and more flustered. What must Mr Allen think of her? It was surely only too obvious to him by now that she had bluffed her way into the ball by pretending to be a tourist, and that her real intention had been to meet Alex Gillon—who equally obviously hadn't wanted to meet her.

Anger at Alex Gillon's attitude mingled with her acute embarrassment. She had an urge to launch into him and tell him off for this cruel indifference to his family and background, and an equally strong urge to melt away fast before things grew any stickier. Her pride made her stay put, and a raw fighting spirit that she had barely known she possessed sent her on to the offensive.

'I guess Mr Gillon doesn't like to think of himself as an immigrant, Mr Allen,' she said in a taut voice. 'But if you're proud of your English ancestors, I don't see why he should be ashamed of his.'

'I sure ain't ashamed,' Alex replied, in a south-western drawl that sounded to her ears to be deliberately exaggerated. 'But I'm a New Mexican now. England don't mean any more to me than it means to Kent here, or Darlene, or anyone else in this town. This state, even.'

'That can hardly be true, Mr Gillon, when you still have relations living there.'

'Alex, does this mean you're a natural-born Englishman?' Kent Allen asked curiously.

'Yeah, I was born there but, as I said, New Mexico's my home now.'

'Then you ought to be able to talk with a real neat English accent, like Lady Laura here.' Darlene giggled.

'No way.' Alex Gillon forced a cold smile, but Laura had no doubt that underneath it his blood was simmering just like her own. Their politeness was the thinnest of veils over what threatened to erupt into a public argument. 'I've been over here too long for that. Kent, I wanted a word with you before the dinner starts. Excuse us, folks.'

It should have been a relief to Laura that he had found an excuse to cut off their confrontation, but her first thought—and her second too—was that he was once again slipping out of her grasp. She felt she couldn't stay on at the ball any longer, now that her cover had been blown. She had to come away with something from this encounter if she wasn't to go back to England empty-handed.

'Mr Gillon,' she called desperately after him, as he began to move away.

The face that he turned back to her showed his annoyance with brutal clarity, but she pushed on anyway. 'Mr Gillon, I have some business that I really must discuss with you while I'm in town. Could I have a word with you later?'

'Not tonight.' He scowled, his brows a firm line above his darkened eyes. 'Come to my office at seven-thirty tomorrow. You know where it is.'

'Seven-thirty in the morning?'

'You heard.' He turned away again, this time so decisively that she could not possibly have challenged him again.

People were already starting to seat themselves at the long tables in the ballroom. Laura hesitated, feeling that she really ought to find Susie-Jo Allen and apologise before returning to her room. And just then Mrs Allen appeared, looking sunny-faced and completely unaware of the scene she had just missed.

'Our table's over there, at the far side.'

'Mrs Allen, I think I ought to leave. I'm a stranger here, and I really shouldn't have——'

'Nonsense,' Mrs Allen said firmly. 'Everybody's dying to talk to you. Darlene Dixon said you know friends of Alex Gillon's in *England*? Boy, we've known Alex for so long, and we never knew he was born English!'

'I guess it's something he prefers not to discuss.'

'Maybe, but I'll tell you, I'm curious!' Mrs Allen smiled, then noticed Laura's tense expression, and rapidly added, 'Though I guess my curiosity might have to wait till another time. You come and tell us all about England, anyway. It's this way.'

Laura gave in, and let the other woman lead her over to the table. It was already crowded, and she found herself seated next to the computer boss she had met earlier, with an empty chair at her other side. Soon her neighbours were deluging her with questions about how she liked New Mexico, and what she had seen so far.

The first course was being served—a spicy crab dish—when Kent Allen and Alex Gillon reappeared. Kent took his place next to his wife, further up the table, and Laura realised with a sinking heart that Alex would be sitting next to her.

But she wasn't destined to have too much of his attention, since Darlene Dixon, fluttery and flirty, was on his other side. One of the men opposite asked about

Alex's English birth, but he answered tersely and coldly, and the question wasn't raised again.

The meal was vast, and excellent. A steak the size of a cartwheel was accompanied by a gigantic salad, and followed by an ice-cream dessert large enough to sink a battleship. Though wine was offered, many people continued to drink cocktails throughout the meal. Laura, already tired, tried not to drink too much, and she couldn't help noticing that Alex Gillon, too, rarely let his glass be refilled.

She couldn't help noticing Alex Gillon, full stop. His physical presence was even more powerful now that she was trapped at his side. He didn't speak directly to her at all, but inevitably he was drawn into one or two cross-table conversations in which she too was involved, and she cast several covert glances at him while he was talking to Darlene.

He was much taller than Lord Exonby, even allowing for the fact that the earl was bent almost double now by arthritis. But the air of vigour that they both gave off seemed to be a family trait, and so was the leonine mane of hair that sprung up and back from Alex's forehead. His face was tanned and weather-beaten, doubtless the result of much exposure to the hot New Mexico sun, but the sharp profile, with a hawklike curve to his nose, was already familiar to her. He didn't sound like an English aristocrat, but in a black dinner-jacket and white shirt he wouldn't have looked out of place presiding at a banquet at Exonby Hall.

Which was what he could and should have been doing, she thought with renewed irritation. Why didn't he intend to come back to England? Why couldn't he have responded at least with some attempt at charm when the Exonbys wrote to him? And, above all, why should he be so annoyed at her own appearance? It was abundantly clear now that he wished she hadn't come to New

Mexico, but why? She wasn't a debt collector or a muck-raking journalist, she had only come to ask him to return to discuss his future inheritance. What was so terrible about that, to make him react with instant, barely concealed anger?

He had obviously told nobody in this town of his English background, and equally obviously he had been annoyed that she should have mentioned it herself. But why? It was no cause for shame, far from it. He should have been as proud of his distinguished family as she was of hers. From the way she herself had been welcomed, he might have known that people here would be curious, rather than critical, if they knew about it—so why did he mind? He seemed to be on the defensive, but why, when she didn't have any weapons to attack him with?

She couldn't understand it. And she wasn't going to waste an enjoyable evening in trying to understand it, she told herself firmly, turning her back on him and fixing her attention on her other neighbours at the table.

Coffee came round. Then Susie-Jo Allen rose, to shouts of 'Silence', and gave a brief speech of thanks to all those who had contributed to the local charity fund. She did it well, Laura thought, envying the effortless self-confidence that all American women seemed to wear like a second skin.

To her surprise, it was Alex who rose to thank Susie-Jo, and to go on to give a short speech himself. While Susie-Jo's had been earnest, Alex's was a more humorous speech, sharply delivered. Most of the jokes were about local characters, and Laura couldn't follow them, but she could tell from the laughter and applause that his satire was accurately aimed.

It was an admirable effort, but it left her even more confused than before. Was this really the Alex Gillon whom Lord Exonby had described as 'thick as two short planks', and whom Anthony had said fell apart whenever you put a pen in his hand? He didn't strike her as remotely slow-witted. His look, his manner, his speech, his successful career—everything spoke of a clever, determined and brilliantly successful man. And yet she had come to New Mexico expecting to dig out a mumbling garage mechanic!

The Exonbys will be relieved, she couldn't help thinking. He's an heir they would be proud to introduce to anybody. Then she sneaked another look at his implacable profile, as he sat down again to tumultuous applause and turned to whisper something to Darlene, and she remembered that she hadn't yet even begun to persuade him to come back to Exonby with her.

Offering this man the fare to London obviously wouldn't act as an inducement in the slightest. But was there anything at all that would persuade him to come with her when she returned? He seemed to have everything he could want already, and he had already made clear his antipathy to England and things English, her included. After that first trite compliment to a 'beautiful lady', he had made no attempt even to be minimally pleasant to her.

Just then the band struck up, and the man on her other side asked her to dance, so she pushed away her thoughts and rapidly accepted the invitation. He was followed by such a succession of other partners that Laura rarely had a moment to sit down. She soon got used to the slow drawl of the local speech, and to being called 'Lady Mallingham'—with the accent firmly on the 'ham'! In between dances, a stream of men and women came across to introduce themselves to her and invite her to visit them while she was in town. How different it all was from England, she thought—but how refreshing, too, particularly in contrast to Alex Gillon's implacable hostility.

Laura's enjoyment was only marred when she was invited to dance by a thin, greasy-haired man who seemed to be all hands. Whenever one drifted downwards from her waist, she would reach down and firmly move it back up—only to have the process start again a moment later. Finally she lost patience, and hissed at him, 'Do stop that!' The man laughed, leaned closer to her, and whispered in her ear a suggestion of such astonishing crudeness that she could hardly believe what she was hearing.

'Excuse me, Art,' a familiar, harsh voice cut in. 'I promised Lady Laura this dance.'

Any rescuer was welcome just then, even if she would have preferred almost anyone else to Alex Gillon. Art, muttering and casting black looks, slunk away, and after a momentary hesitation Laura moved into Alex's waiting arms.

'Don't mind Art,' he said quietly, leading her smoothly into the dance. 'He's a damn menace, but it's all talk and no action with him.'

'Englishmen don't talk like that.'

'This is a different country, honey.'

'How right you are.'

He didn't immediately reply to this, and after a moment Laura risked a comment on the weather. But this drew a monosyllabic reply, and she realised that he had no intention of pursuing the kind of light conversation her other partners had kept up. She didn't really mind; it was a relief to pause from chatter, and a relief to know that Alex's hostility wasn't so total as to keep him from offering her a token dance.

And a rather enjoyable dance it was, too. The band was playing a slow waltz number, and all over the floor couples were swaying in time to the music. Alex was a very competent dancer. His hands rested firmly on her shoulders, holding her loosely to him, and she couldn't help being conscious of the hard warmth of his body, and the faint spicy smell that came from him.

What an attractive man he is, she thought through a haze of wine and weariness. Eligible too, even if you discount Exonby and the title. Lucky Darlene. Mind you, if she hasn't got him to the altar in ten years he must have a fair resistance to her. Maybe he has been married to someone else? She wished she knew more about those missing years of his life.

The music wound to a close, and their feet slowed. Laura raised her eyes and looked at Alex. He was a good six inches taller than she was, even in her highest-heeled sandals. He looked back at her, not with a scowl now, but with an almost gentle expression. The current of attraction that she had felt earlier was just as strong as before, but now it seemed less harsh, more—more erotic.

For the first time all evening, she felt a sudden sensation of her feminine power. He's attracted to me just as strongly as I am to him, she thought. All right, he wishes nobody had come to beg him to return to Exonby, but he isn't hostile to me personally. In fact, quite the opposite. Perhaps I could charm him into agreeing after all.

'If you say another damn word to anyone about my family in England, I'll make sure you're railroaded out of this town in the morning.'

As he finished this speech the band struck up again, and for a moment, her attention distracted to the dance, Laura didn't take in its sense. Then she realised how aggressive his words had been, how far her optimistic hopes were from being achieved, and she instinctively pulled away from him.

His hands, rough now on her shoulders, promptly hauled her back. He started to move again, keeping time unobtrusively with the music.

'Maybe you reckon it makes no difference to me what you say about them,' he went on in the same low but firm voice, 'but I'm telling you it does.'

Laura took a couple of deep breaths, succeeded in burying her angry disappointment, and found her tongue. 'But why? Why? They're nothing to be ashamed of.'

'My background's no business of anyone here. No business of yours, neither.'

'It's the business I've come here for.'

'Then keep it to yourself until the morning.'

She didn't answer. They drifted nearer the band. Alex was dancing slowly, his hands loose on her again, but she somehow couldn't alter his course, she could only flow with it, as if the taut competence of his movements paralysed her. Earlier she had been enjoying the sensation of being swept along by him, but now it annoyed her. She had thought she was getting through to him a little, but all she had done was lower her guard, and let him get through to her!

'I want you to promise,' he said in a harsh but low voice.

Slowly, almost reluctantly, she brought her eyes up to meet his once more. He held her look firmly, implacably. This wasn't the charming womaniser that she had sensed for a moment earlier; this look was pure tycoon.

'I won't say anything tonight,' she said grudgingly. 'I'll be going in a few minutes, anyway.'

'I'll hold you to that.'

'I promise.' She loaded this comment with scorn that he should doubt her earlier word.

'Even so, I'm staying with you till you leave.'

'Thank you, sir!'

His fingernails dug into her shoulders, as if he was reminding her that people were casting curious glances at them. It must be obvious that they were arguing, Laura thought suddenly, and everybody in the big room was probably wondering what they were arguing about. Alex Gillon might put off the questions until the next day, but before long everybody would be grilling him about his mysterious English relatives. Still, he seemed more than sharp enough to realise that, and to work out his own ways of diverting their questions.

Even so, it seemed that she did after all have the power to embarrass him. He wouldn't like it one bit if she let it drop that he was the future Earl of Exonby. If all else failed, she thought hazily, perhaps she would play that card.

The music stopped. 'Let's find Susie-Jo,' Alex said.

They found her easily, talking with an elderly lady in a quiet corner. Laura didn't need to lie about her tiredness, she really was falling asleep on her feet, and Susie-Jo readily accepted her excuse that jet lag would keep her from staying any later. Five minutes later she was back in her room, and it was all she could do to undress and wash quickly before she fell asleep.

When Laura woke, bright sunlight was streaming through the windows of her room. Curse it, she had forgotten to shut the curtains the night before! Then she glanced at her watch, and realised it was just as well that the sun had woken her. She had also forgotten to rebook her morning call after making her arrangement to meet Alex Gillon, and she was due in his office in just over half an hour!

Luckily it didn't take her too long to shower, comb through her hair and fasten it back, and slip on a strappy sun-dress in pale blue chambray and blue sandals to match. As the traffic downtown was light, it was barely seven twenty-five when she slipped into a parking space a block away from the Northways building. The recep-

tionist wasn't yet at work, but a porter let her in and
saw her into the lift to the top floor.

The secretary Gloria wasn't at work either, but the
doors to Alex Gillon's office were open, and when Laura
peeped through them she saw Alex himself, in dark grey
suit trousers and a short-sleeved white shirt, standing at
his desk with a telephone receiver in one hand.

He glanced round and motioned her to come in, then
turned away to concentrate on his phone call. Laura
stepped in, a little nervously, and looked around.

She had barely glimpsed his office yesterday, but now
she had time for a more careful look. His desk was a
slab of solid granite, dramatic and expensive. The easy
chairs were covered in soft hide, and the painting on the
wall looked to be an original Monet. She examined this
for a few minutes, then crossed to the window and looked
out. She could see right across the town, from the office
blocks of downtown to the flat roofs and telegraph poles
of the suburbs, the brownish trickle of the river in a
dusty, deep-sided bed, and the long pale streak of the
highway cutting across the rocky scrubland beyond.

She tried not to give Alex more than the occasional
glance, but she was very conscious of him, standing
barely three or four paces away from her. His voice was
loud, harsh and confident, his stance confident, too. His
bare arms were deeply tanned, and lightly covered with
hair bleached pale by the strong sun. His watch was steel,
businesslike rather than showy. He did not glance towards her again.

The office, Alex's harsh voice, his whole manner,
seemed to reinforce the impression of him as a powerful,
influential, sharply decisive man. She hadn't had time
to get really nervous before coming to his office, but she
found this wait unnerving. Lady Exonby was wrong, she
thought. It's no use acting like an English lady towards
this man. That will do nothing but arouse his hostility.

I need to behave like the Americans he's used to, the kind of clever salesmen he deals with every day, or he'll brush off my approaches without a second thought.

Finally he came to the end of his call, rang off, and turned to confront her. Their eyes met for the first time that morning. His were alert and slightly narrowed. Laura held them for several seconds, but he seemed determined to stare her out, and she wasn't inclined to engage in silent battles with him before their meeting had even begun, so she dropped her gaze and moved a half-step backwards. He must have stayed at the ball far later than she had done, but he showed no sign of tiredness or of a hangover.

'Coffee?'

That was better—it was almost a sign that he was human after all! 'Thank you,' she said, with a relief she didn't attempt to hide. 'I'd love one. White with no sugar, please.'

He went out to Gloria's territory, and a few moments later returned with two cups, one of which he held out to her. 'I've only fifteen minutes,' he said.

'It's barely a quarter to eight, for heaven's sake.'

'The business day starts at eight round here. I want you out by then.'

'Then I'll be as brief as I can.' She said it forcefully, in as American a manner as she could muster. She put her cup down on the low table, and—without waiting to be asked—sat in one of the chairs that clustered around it. She opened her briefcase and drew out Lady Exonby's buff file. She spread this open on her knees, then looked up, and went on, 'You've read the letter from Lord Exonby that I brought yesterday.'

'Uh-huh.'

'Then it'll be clear to you that it's necessary for you to come back to Exonby. Even if you don't plan to settle there permanently, you must come and discuss everything with the earl and countess.'

Alex Gillon shook his head. He took a sip of his coffee, then he bent to put his cup down next to hers and, turning his back to her, walked towards the window. Laura watched him. He moved economically, and not at all clumsily, but there was a tautness about him that kept his movements from being graceful.

He's nervous too, she thought suddenly. Tense. That harsh edge to his voice betrays it too. Alex Gillon might be a powerful man, but he isn't a relaxed one. Is that because of me and my errand, or is he always like this? She couldn't decide which was the case.

He set his hands in his trouser pockets, spreading his weight a little, and didn't turn round. 'I'm a busy man,' he said. 'A trip to England is out of the question.'

'It needn't be a long trip. Even a week would be better than nothing.'

'A week? A week!' He let out a short, terse laugh, then spun round to confront her. 'You know how long it is since I was last away from here for a week?'

'Far too long, I should think,' Laura retorted, with a bluntness that surprised her as soon as the words were out. She went on, hurriedly, before she lost impetus, 'Nobody ought to be indispensable in a company this size. It looks to me as if you could do with a good holiday. Why not take one in England, and visit Exonby at the same time?'

'You think going to England would be a *holiday*?'

'Why not? Gloucestershire is a beautiful county, and Exonby itself is lovely. The house is famous for its elegant architecture, and the park too is beautiful. You must remember it a little, even if it is twenty years since you were there. And Lord and Lady Exonby would be delighted to see you.'

'That's junk. They'd go through the motions, but they always shivered in their shoes at the thought of the place passing to me.'

She had to steel herself not to recoil at the venom in Alex's voice. He spoke as if he hated the Exonbys, really hated them.

He couldn't, he mustn't! They were such kind, gentle people; they weren't his enemies! She opened her mouth to contradict him, but then it struck her that easy, empty assurances wouldn't carry any weight with this man at all. His hatred was clearly genuine, and he had to have some reason for feeling so strongly.

What could it be? Something from his childhood presumably, something from those days when he'd been an antisocial tearaway who'd barely avoided being expelled from school. No, the Exonbys wouldn't have liked that. Perhaps they really had shown him hostility at that time, and he remembered and resented it still.

It seemed a petty motive to govern a powerful man's actions for twenty years and more, but she could think of no other explanation.

'I shouldn't think they relished it when you were a boy,' she said thoughtfully. 'You were quite a tearaway, by all accounts, and they must have had reason for their doubts about you. But that's all the more cause for you to come back now. They've heard nothing about you since you came over here, and to be honest they've been afraid you'd gone completely to the dogs. You've obviously done quite the reverse, though. Once they hear what a success you've made over here they'll be ever so relieved. And they'll be more than happy, I'm sure, to put Exonby in your hands.'

Alex didn't reply. He put his hands in his trouser pockets, and leaned back against the thick plate glass of the window. Behind him, the sun blazed down, more and more strongly, on the harsh, infertile countryside of New Mexico.

Laura watched him in silence. She didn't like this pause; she would have preferred to keep their conversation going and avoid having time to think about how much he unnerved her. She wasn't used to men like him. He seemed almost to be at one with the hostile countryside outside the window, as stern and sharp and unforgiving as the cacti and rock. The country she was used to—and the men she was used to, too—were so totally different.

These thoughts brought her naturally to think of Exonby. Even in midsummer, it wasn't an oven like this place. She could see in her mind an English cloudy day, the greenness of the Gloucestershire countryside, the roses in the walled garden at Exonby, and the apples and pears growing in the orchard. An English river, full and gently flowing, willow trees, and cricket on the lawns.

'Don't you miss it even a tiny bit?' she said dreamily.

'England? God, no. Never.' He moved again, jerkily, coming to stand over her. He set his arms on the back of the chair opposite hers, and leaned forward, fixing her with his pale brown eyes.

'Look, you must understand, Lady Laura. There's no way I'm coming back to England. Not for a week, not even for a day. Certainly not forever. I meant what I wrote them. I don't give a damn what they do with the estate.'

'For heaven's sake, Mr Gillon! It's not a cottage garden! You're set to inherit five thousand acres of prime Gloucestershire farmland, worth millions of pounds!'

Alex stared at her for a moment, then he straightened up, threw back his head and laughed, harshly. 'Five thousand acres! Do you have any idea how much land I own out here?'

'It might be a million acres for all I care, but Exonby's still your responsibility.'

'Not yet it isn't.'

'It will be soon enough, and with a place like Exonby you can't just step in overnight. You need to get to know the estate, the tenants, the servants, to make sure there'll be a smooth transition.'

'A smooth transition!' Alex laughed again. 'Good God, you really think it'll reassure them if I come over, don't you?'

'I'm certain it will.'

'Then let me tell you something, Lady Laura.' He leaned forward once more, rocking the chair slightly, and frowned for a moment. His voice lowered. He wasn't laughing now, he was completely serious.

'Yes, I remember Exonby,' he said. 'Of course I do. I must have been there twenty, thirty times when I was a boy. I remember that goddamn barn of a house, and those rolling lawns, and Moxon's Wood, and the marshes down by Whitehouse Farm. I remember the valets and the butler and the Master of Foxhounds and the whole damn paraphernalia of nineteenth-century England. And I know—how could I not know? It was drummed into me hard enough—that the whole lot has to come to me. I also know that the entail stops with me, and I can do with it just as I like.

'I know how much it's worth, give or take a million, and I know exactly what I'll do with it. If I can sell it lock, stock and barrel then that's what I'll do. If I don't find any takers I'll apply to have the house knocked down, and if I can't do that I'll apply to have it turned into apartments. I'll fire the servants and sell the park for farmland. I'll sell the farms and the woodland and the shooting rights and every other damn thing the Exonbys possess. Oh, don't worry, I'll leave Lady Exonby her precious Dower House and her rose garden.

But I don't want to live in that house like the Exonbys do now. And I won't—I won't even try to—keep the place going as it is.

'I'll drag the whole damn estate into the late twentieth century, kicking and screaming if need be. What's more, I'll do it all from here, without coming within a thousand miles of the place. I don't want ever to see Exonby Hall again. You think it'll reassure the Exonbys to hear that?'

'I think if you saw Exonby again, you might change your mind.'

'Then you don't know me, Lady Laura. You don't know me at all.'

She tried to think of an answer, an argument to use against him, but the flat decisiveness of his speech had taken all her certainty away. This wasn't a man she could beg or wheedle into doing as she chose: Alex Gillon had already thought out his position, and she knew it wouldn't be easy to shift him from it.

'Mr Gillon?' a voice interrupted them.

He straightened once more, abruptly, and Laura jumped to her feet.

'Morning, Gloria,' Alex said.

Gloria came from the doorway, right into the room. 'Oh.' She stopped in her tracks. 'I didn't realise you had a visitor.'

'Lady Laura's just going.'

She didn't dare to argue with him in front of Gloria, and she knew, too, that it would have been useless to argue further even if Gloria had not interrupted them. She wasn't used to confrontations like this. She was no good at them. The Exonbys should have sent somebody else, she thought miserably; she was going to have to go back and admit total failure. But could anyone else have done any better? Most likely not, she thought, though it was cold comfort just then.

'May I finish my coffee first?'

'Sure,' Alex said offhandedly. 'I'll be with you in five minutes, Gloria.'

Five minutes. Could she use it? Was there anything else she could say? Her mind seemed to have gone blank. She took a sip of the coffee, her eyes carefully averted from Alex. She expected him to stride away and busy himself with his papers or something to make it clear that their conversation was over, but he didn't; she was very conscious of him standing close to her, watching her.

Slowly, reluctantly, she looked up at him.

'I'm sorry,' he said awkwardly, 'that you've wasted your journey.'

'So am I.'

There was a short pause, then Laura went on tentatively, 'Doesn't the title mean anything to you? Anything at all?'

'No.' He eyed her curiously, then said in an oddly gentle voice, 'You can't understand that, can you?'

'No, I can't. Not at all. How can you not care about your family history? How can you be so—so cold about it all? Don't you know there have been Gillons at Exonby for over four hundred years? It's a wonderful tradition, and I just can't understand how you can break it so callously, without thinking it over in the slightest.'

'I have thought it over,' Alex retorted more brusquely. The corners of his mouth turned down, and for a moment she glimpsed what she took to be a deep bitterness in his expression. But when he spoke, it was not with bitterness, but with a biting contempt so powerful that she felt herself cringe away from him. 'The English class system,' he said venomously. 'It stinks, you know that? I said just now that the title doesn't mean anything, but that isn't really true. It means plenty to me, and I hate every damn thing it stands for.'

'But——' Laura began, but Alex gave her no chance to interrupt.

He went on remorselessly, 'Oh, I know it impresses people. You gave me a good demonstration of that last night, didn't you? People like Kent and Susie-Jo, fine folks who are worth a dozen of you, crawling all over you just because you told them you were "Lady" Laura. It's sickening, false and sickening. I don't want that kind of approval, don't want it and don't need it. People here respect me for what I've done myself, not what my ancestors did. That's the way I plan to keep it.'

'You still would be respected for what you've achieved,' Laura said desperately. Her face was flaming in response to his vicious personal attack, but she tried to ignore her embarrassment. 'It won't take anything away from what you've done here when you become an earl. But that's—that's what has been ordained for you. What you were born to.'

'Born to?' Alex laughed again, brusquely. 'At best it's an accident of fate. If Lady Exonby had had a son, or if old George had divorced or outlived her and married again, I wouldn't have been *born* to it, would I? What on earth do you imagine I ought to have done with my life? Hung around Exonby, playing polo and drinking cherry brandy and praying the old goat wouldn't get himself a son in his old age? No, thank you!'

'Well, no. I can understand why you came here. But now that you're certain to inherit——'

'Now I'm nudging forty. I'm settled here. I've been here half my lifetime and there's no way, no way at all, I'm coming back to England.'

'So what shall I tell the Exonbys?'

'If I were you,' Alex said bluntly, 'I'd tell them the truth.'

'Obviously I will. But I still wish that the truth were different.'

'We all wish that sometimes, honey, but it ain't.'

There was a tone of finality in Alex's voice now. Laura reached for her cup, and drained the last mouthful of coffee. She was racking her brains for another argument that she might use, but they seemed to have been blasted empty by his onslaught.

'Well, thank you for talking to me, Mr Gillon,' she said resignedly.

'That's OK. I'm only sorry I was so sharp with you yesterday. But you have to understand, I have problems of my own over here, and I don't want the whole weight of Exonby dumped on me as well.'

But it isn't a weight! Laura thought. It's a beautiful, glorious place, and it should be a pleasure and a privilege to you to inherit it. You obviously don't see it like that, though, and I don't know how else to try to change your mind.

They shook hands formally. Rather to her surprise, Alex didn't hand her over to Gloria, but walked with her to the lift, and waited by her side while it was coming. It took less than a minute to arrive, and she stepped in as soon as the doors opened, but he put a hard hand on the edge of the door, and leaned forward to talk to her where she stood inside.

'You staying here long?'

'I'm not sure. I'll be here tonight, obviously. Perhaps I'll stay another day or two. I've come so far, and I don't suppose I'll ever be back this way again. I might as well look at the Carlsbad Caverns at least.'

'You should. They're impressive, really impressive.'

'So I've heard.'

'Are you busy this evening?'

'I'm not sure.' This small talk struck her as embarrassingly out of place after the vehemence of their earlier discussion, but ingrained habit made her dredge up a polite half-smile and go on, 'I received so many invitations last night, and I honestly don't know which of them will get followed up today!'

'Have dinner with me tonight.'

Her eyes widened. Have dinner with him! He couldn't be serious! But his unwavering look trapped and held hers, and what she read in it left her in no doubt that he was.

'I warn you, there's no way I'll discuss Exonby again,' he said. 'But I wouldn't want you to feel we've made you unwelcome here. Stay a few days and look around. Northways will foot your bill. Take your own advice, give yourself a holiday. Maybe then you'll get to see why I like the place so much.'

He wasn't scowling now, he was smiling, openly and relaxedly. The smile transformed his face, making him look younger, nearly boyish. Almost unconsciously, Laura found herself smiling back, not superficially, but with a feeling of genuine warmth towards this prickly but forthright man.

'Maybe I will.'

'You're staying at the Marbury? I'll pick you up at six.'

'Six?'

'That's the usual time for dinner round these parts.'

How little she knew! Laura thought, as she drove back to the motel. Work at eight; dinner at six. She'd thought she had seen so many American films that she knew just what to expect, but little differences like this timing of the day's events seemed to catch her out at every turn.

And Alex Gillon himself was so different, so very, very different from the rebellious kid that Anthony and the Exonbys had described to her that she didn't know how to begin to tell them all about him.

He seemed so totally at home in New Mexico that it really was hard to imagine him growing up as an English public schoolboy. But then, she thought, that defiant boy must still lurk somewhere underneath his weather-beaten exterior.

He still remembered Exonby. She recalled his voice when he had spoken about the estate. There had been contempt there, true, but there had been something else as well. For a moment, just a moment, the Yankee accent had slipped, and she had heard the faint echo in his voice of an English upper-class accent.

Give her another three or four hours with him that evening, she thought, and she might yet manage to get somewhere with him.

CHAPTER FOUR

LAURA spent most of that day in the hotel, swimming and sunbathing by the pool. She felt she needed the rest, after a couple of days in which she had barely stopped still, and she certainly enjoyed the sunshine, coming from a rather wet English summer.

At five to six her room telephone rang to tell her that Alex Gillon had arrived, and she hurried down to the reception to meet him. She hadn't been certain what to wear for their dinner, and had finally picked a simple cream shift and high-heeled sandals, made dressier by a wide gold belt and the jewellery she had worn the evening before.

For a moment she couldn't see Alex. Then she recognised his tall figure—and did a double take. The previous evening he had been sophisticated in dinner-jacket and bow-tie; tonight he was wearing pink and white striped trousers and a bright turquoise short-sleeved shirt.

'Hi,' he said, coming over to her.

'Hi,' she echoed nervously. It wasn't a word she normally used, but she couldn't think what else to say. Alex Gillon stunned her, he paralysed her. Her mind and her tongue didn't seem to work in his presence, or to work only in strange and unpredictable ways. She thought, suddenly, of Anthony's warning, and knew immediately that this was what he had warned her of, this intense, barely controllable attraction to the man in front of her.

Strangely, the thought was comforting. This isn't something that affects just me, she thought to herself;

it's the effect that Alex Gillon has on every woman. So there's no point in my taking much notice of it—and he certainly won't be affected in the same way!

'Do you want a drink here before we go on?' Alex asked.

'Yes, please, but I don't know what to order. Can you suggest something?'

'Try a Tom Collins. That's long and cool, gin and lemony.'

'That should do very nicely.'

Laura sat at a table by the entrance to the bar, and watched him stride over to order their drinks. How—how very *American* he looked! A couple of days in New Mexico had told her plenty about the American preference for leisure clothes with bright colours and strong patterns, but somehow she hadn't imagined that Alex Gillon would share it. But he couldn't be taken for an upper-class Englishman tonight; he looked like a typical local businessman relaxing on an evening out.

The Tom Collins came in a tall glass solid with crushed ice—as was Alex's own drink. 'Mine's neat Coke,' he said shortly. 'I'm driving. I thought we'd go down to Carlsbad, if you can spare the time. It's a bigger town, and more of a tourist resort, so there's a much better choice of restaurants round about.'

'Is it far?'

'Thirty miles or so. Won't take us long down the freeway.'

Thirty miles for supper! That wasn't any too English either, but Alex's tone of voice made it clear that it was nothing exceptional round here. 'Do you like Mexican food?' he went on.

'I tried some on my first evening here, in Albuquerque. I had—oh, what was it called?'

'Chilli? Tacos? Enchiladas?'

'Enchiladas, that's it.'

'That's Mexican fast food,' Alex told her. 'It's fine in its way, but I was thinking of a place that does classier stuff: fish, and meat dishes that aren't so heavy on the refried beans.'

'OK, I'll trust you,' she agreed with a smile. 'Do you eat out a lot?'

'Most evenings I either eat with friends, or grab a quick meal in one of the local diners. I have a house-keeper, but I don't like to eat alone at home.'

'You're not married?'

'No, never have been.'

She felt herself relax, as if this information had come as a relief to her, and immediately she recognised the feeling she could have kicked herself. What was it to her if Alex Gillon was, or had been, married? Nothing, nothing at all! She was Sir Anthony Downing's fiancée and this man's private life had nothing to do with her. She reminded herself very firmly that this dinner together was no more than Alex would have offered to any business associate who had come to the town to see him, and to cover her confusion she went on rapidly and lightly, 'It runs in the family, I guess.'

'What does?'

'Not marrying—or, at least, marrying late.'

A cloud of annoyance seemed to mar the clear, angular lines of Alex's face, and she knew that it had been the wrong thing to say. 'Lady Exonby told me your father married late in life,' she added by way of explanation. Alex might think that she had been prying unnecessarily into his background, but that was just his prickliness, she thought to herself; really her job gave her every right to know as much as she did about him, and far more!

'True,' Alex said blankly. Then he forced a smile, and continued, 'How about you? Do you have a husband back in England?'

'Not yet, but I will soon. I'm engaged—I have been since Christmas. We're planning to get married later this year. Actually you may remember my fiancé, since he told me you were at school together. His name's Anthony Downing. I suppose it was plain Anthony Downing in those days, but now he's Sir Anthony Downing.'

She said this with pride, but Alex repeated 'Downing?' in a puzzled voice accompanied by a half-frown, and the pride faded like morning mist. She knew what Anthony's opinion of Alex Gillon had been, but it hadn't occurred to her before to wonder what Alex would have made of Anthony as a schoolboy. Now she did wonder, and the thought made her oddly uncomfortable.

'Perhaps you won't remember him.' After all, she reminded herself, you're the man who claims barely to remember his own aunt and uncle. 'He's a couple of years older than you. Tallish, brown-haired, rather quiet.'

'Oh, *Downing*!' A hint of that underlying public-school accent crept back into Alex's voice, and with it a dismissive note.

For a ghastly, traitorous moment she knew why. She could just envisage Anthony as a big, clumsy schoolboy, earnest and humourless and disapproving of all Alex's high spirits and wild pranks. Of course, Alex would have felt nothing but contempt for boring, colourless Downing.

But that only showed up *his* limitations, she told herself. Anthony's qualities might not be showy, but they were sterling none the less. Anthony was steady, dependable, capable, considerate, and far more that was just as admirable. Alex Gillon might not understand the worth of loyalty, love of tradition, security, but she understood it very well herself. Those were the most important things in life—and the reasons why she had chosen Anthony as her future husband.

'He's a fine man,' she said in a quiet, firm voice. She couldn't leave this arrogant phoenix of a man to think disparagingly of her beloved Anthony. Anyone with sense could see that Anthony was ten times the man Alex Gillon was. She smiled a proud, private smile and went on, 'Anthony runs Maltwood—his family estate in Gloucestershire, not far from Exonby—and he's a member of Lloyd's, too.'

'Sounds like a solid, conventional choice. I guess your parents approve.'

'Of course they do.' It was true; they did, whole-heartedly. 'They both like Anthony very much.'

'Jolly good show.'

Alex's voice was only a shade removed from parody. It hit Laura like a blow that she hadn't persuaded him in the slightest. He still thought of Downing as a nobody, and he wasn't remotely impressed by her choice. Her anger began to flare, but before she could snap back at him he rose to his feet. 'We'd better be moving. I booked for seven-thirty.'

Stiff with annoyance, Laura followed him out to the motel forecourt. 'That's mine,' he said, gesturing to a low-slung, shiny dark blue sports car, and striding towards it.

So it would be, she thought furiously. Mentally she contrasted it with Anthony's battered Range Rover. Mentally she costed it. Alex Gillon is every bit as snobbish as any conventional aristocrat, she told herself, it's just that money is the only value he understands. He despises Anthony, whom he hasn't seen for years and knows nothing about, simply because he guesses that Anthony hasn't made a million. Well, he hasn't, but it isn't as if that's the only important thing in life!

She hated herself for admiring the elegant lines of the car, and the butter-smooth leather of the seat into which she slid. She didn't look at Alex once as he manoeuvred out of the forecourt and drove on to the freeway.

If Alex noticed her renewed hostility, he didn't mention it. For some minutes they sat in silence, then he said in a cool voice, 'Put on some music if you'd like to. I don't care to talk while I drive.'

Laura found that understandable, since there was a steady, fast-moving stream of traffic on the freeway. All the same she didn't want to obey him, but after a few minutes more the silence, broken only by the purr of the engine and the low hiss of the air-conditioner, began to seem oppressive, and she reached for the pile of cassettes on the dashboard.

Doubtless he would have ghastly taste in music, she told herself, and there would be nothing at all that she could face listening to. But she was mistaken. The recordings were mainly of classical works, mostly by Mozart and Berlioz, who were among her own favourite composers. She selected Mozart's Clarinet Concerto, and soon the familiar haunting notes had begun to soothe her ruffled sensibilities.

She glanced at Alex, for just long enough to see that his own gaze was fixed firmly on the road ahead. Then she glanced again; then, bolder, she took a long, careful look at his firm profile.

She could see it now. She could see the resemblance to Lord Exonby quite unmistakably; more, she could guess how he must have looked as that rebellious schoolboy, twenty years before. But at the same time he looked perfectly at home in his new setting. If she hadn't known about his background, and hadn't been looking for shades of the English aristocrat in his appearance, she would have taken him without a second thought to be a lifelong inhabitant of the American Deep South.

As the Allens had done, she thought to herself, and Darlene Dixon, and the receptionist at Northways, and all the rest of Alex Gillon's long-term American associates. None of those people had been instantly struck by Alex's blue blood. They didn't think in those terms at all. To them, he was just another American—an unusually determined and successful one, but differing from the mass in nothing more than that.

Was that how he saw himself? She couldn't believe it. This man had grown up, from his earliest days, knowing that he would almost certainly inherit Exonby and its earldom. If he had ever felt himself to be special, wasn't it—*mustn't* it have been—for that reason?

'This is the place,' Alex said, pulling into a neon-lit roadhouse just after they had passed across the Carlsbad city boundary. 'It's pretty casual, but the food's fine.'

In fact, though most of the diners were dressed as casually as Alex himself, the restaurant was more formal inside than it had appeared from the road, with low, atmospheric lighting and attentive service from dinner-jacketed waiters. Alex was greeted like an old and valued customer, and the two of them were shown to a table by the window.

They were served first with a selection of dips and crisp corn chips, then with a cold avocado soup. All Alex's persuasion couldn't make Laura try the turkey in chocolate sauce, but his, when it came, looked and smelled so delicious that she almost regretted her refusal. Her own red snapper in a spicy sauce was mouth-watering, though, and, although she couldn't have squeezed in a dessert, she enjoyed the strong coffee that followed.

She had been rather dreading the prospect of having to make polite conversation with Alex for an hour or more, but in fact their talk flowed smoothly. Alex might be capable of forthright aggression, but when he chose to exercise it, she discovered, he also had a great deal of charm.

Laura too was skilled at small talk, and she did her best not to ask Alex any questions that might cause him to take offence. She steered well clear of his personal life, but she risked a general question about Northways, and that proved worthwhile, because he talked readily, and at length, about his career and business during their meal.

He had indeed begun working as a garage mechanic when he had arrived in the States, as Lord Exonby had thought. 'I started in New York,' he explained, 'and kept on moving. I wanted to see the whole country. I worked right across from east to west: Pittsburgh, Chicago, Kansas City, Denver, San Francisco. Had to keep moving at any rate, because I didn't have the right work permits when I started out. But after I'd been here a while I got the recommendations I needed, and then I turned legit.'

'And that's when you came to New Mexico?'

'To Arizona, first. I'd always done two jobs at once, working in a garage by day and a bar by night, and the living's cheap when you're on your own and none too picky. So I'd a few thousand dollars saved up by then, and I took a share in a little garage in Phoenix. My partner there cut and run after a year—just about cleaned me out! But I'd learned my lesson, and when I'd got out from under and saved up some more I started up a repair shop on my own. No more partners, I told myself: from now on I'm going to be the boss.'

'As you are.'

'Right on. Nothing clever about it, just hard work and careful dealing, and seizing the chances when they come your way. In a couple years I had a garage business right across the state. I was making more from car hire than from the sales and repair shops, so I worked on expanding that side of the business. Then I pushed into

New Mexico—this is the next state east from Arizona, right?—and I moved here to keep tabs on things while I was setting the depots up. I got to like the place, so I decided I'd set up my base here, and expand outwards from here when the chances came.'

'And have they come?'

'We've a couple dozen depots in west Texas, and I reckon I'll be spreading a way further before I'm through.'

'You really want to be rich?'

Alex gave a slow smile. 'If I was in England, honey, I'd maybe tell myself I was rich enough already. Hell, I've more than enough money now to buy me all the houses, cars, hot meals and clothes any man could need. But over here, rich ain't enough. Only the poor want to be rich; the rich want to be super-rich.'

'And you're not super-rich yet?'

He shook his head. 'I ain't among the hundred richest men in New Mexico yet, and this is one of the poorest states in the whole damn US of A.'

'It sounds to me as if you're as rich as any man needs to be.'

'Not to me. I want to make my mark on this country before I'm through.' He took a gulp of his coffee. 'You don't approve?'

'Of course I approve. I'm very impressed.'

She said it automatically, knowing that no other reply would have been diplomatic. And it was true, in as far as she was deeply relieved that Alex had proved to be a success in life. But Alex's fixed gaze unnerved her, and brought it home to her, uncomfortably, that it wasn't entirely true. She didn't approve, not when she stopped to contrast what he had done in the States with what he might have done in England. And though she hadn't consciously expressed this feeling, she wasn't really surprised when he leaned forwards across the table to her and said in an intense voice, 'It's not much like farming the ancestral acres back in Gloucestershire. It's business, Laura—and hard, dirty, rough business at that.'

For a moment, she knew just what he meant. She understood what his laconic account hadn't dwelt on, that it had been a long, hard struggle that had turned Alex Gillon the tearaway schoolboy into the toughened, ruthless male who sat opposite her.

And she knew, at the same instant, that she did admire this. That this was what she responded to in him, this strength of character and determination. Her attraction wasn't just physical, it was to his powerful, intensely masculine inner nature.

That thought unnerved her. He was so unlike her father and Anthony and all the Englishmen she knew. She loved and admired them: it didn't seem right, somehow, that she should feel this far more intense pull towards a man who had rejected all that they stood for. Wasn't there just as real a value—different, maybe, but just as positive—in farming the ancestral acres? Of course there was! And it was the weakness in Alex Gillon's attitude, that he seemed totally unable to see it!

'For heaven's sake!' she exclaimed, with a sudden rush of annoyance at his challenge. 'You know what you are? You're an inverted snob! You want me to admire what you've done, and all right, I do! But that doesn't mean you have to despise what Anthony and Lord Exonby and all the rest do, back in England. There's value in their way of life too.'

'Not to my way of thinking.'

'Then you're blind. I don't know why, but somehow you're blind to it all. All you think about is making money, and you can't see the value of a balanced life. You don't seem to understand what family means, what tradition means, what it means to come to terms with your place in society and all that you inherit from your ancestors.'

'Oh, I see England clearly enough,' Alex said grimly. 'And you know what I see, when I look at men like your precious Downing? I see snobbery and self-satisfaction and laziness.'

'Laziness! How dare you, Alex Gillon?'

Laura was stumbling to her feet in her fury, but an imperious wave from Alex's hand set her, almost unconsciously, back in her seat to hear him out. 'Yes, laziness,' he said in a hard but measured voice. 'There are too many men in England who want to make just a tidy bit of money—without getting their hands dirty, mind you, or working so hard that it interferes with their social lives—and then cop out and sit back for the rest of their lives. There are too many money-jugglers and not enough people who make things for themselves. Too many men who expect people to admire them for what their parents were. Well, people can say what they damn well like about my parents, but before I'm through they'll respect me for what I've done myself.'

'You have it all wrong, Alex. Oh, I know there's some point to what you say, but you twist it all round, somehow. It isn't copping out to give time to your family and other aspects of your life. It's the reverse, really it is.'

'It's copping out to live off your ancestors' fat,' Alex persisted. 'Men like Downing don't pay their way in the world, not really pay it. And they know it, which is why they despise people like me who do.'

'They don't! Alex, you're wrong, wrong again! It's generations since the upper classes looked down on tradesmen!'

'How many garage owners do you know, then? How many factory owners? How many shopkeepers, even? Do you know any, any at all? I'll bet all your friends are just like Downing. They're all rich farmers, stock-brokers, merchant bankers and members of Lloyd's. Aren't they?'

'Well, most of them are, yes. But they wouldn't look down on you because you're not, and I don't see why you should look down on them either! Those are all perfectly respectable occupations!'

Alex shook his head. 'You can't see it, can you? I guess I shouldn't expect you to. You're too close. You're a part of the whole rotten system yourself.'

'I'm what? So I'm snobbish, am I? Lazy? Corrupt? My God, Alex Gillon, how long have you known me for, that you dare to damn me so whole-heartedly? Well, I can tell you, snob or not, I'm not staying here a moment longer to be insulted by you!'

Laura slammed her fist on the table, ignoring the curious glances of the other diners, and surged to her feet. She had taken a couple of steps towards the door before she was held back, literally, by Alex's firm grip on her forearm.

'Laura, stop,' he said in an angry voice.

She hadn't much option, not when he was holding her too tightly for her to wrench away. Alex swallowed convulsively, as if he was fighting for a grip on his own temper, then he said more calmly, 'I'm sorry. That was unforgivably rude of me, and I shouldn't have said it. Now please, sit down and finish your coffee, and I promise to behave like a perfect gentleman.'

'I want you to take back what you said.'

She knew from the blank look that came over Alex's face that she was provoking him still more. But she held her ground, and after a moment he said flatly, 'You're quite right. I don't yet know the first thing about you.'

And yet, Laura thought mutinously, you're so firmly convinced I'm a snob that you can't bring yourself directly to withdraw the accusation. Still, it was a climb-down of sorts, and reluctantly she said, 'All right, I accept your apology.'

Alex slowly released her arm, and the two of them resumed their seats.

'Alex,' Laura said earnestly, 'I don't believe I'm a snob, and I don't believe anybody who really knew me could accuse me of being one. But it's certainly true that I'm proud to belong to the Mallingham family, and, come to that, I do think it's right for anyone to take pride in their ancestors' achievements.'

'Not everyone has a family they can be proud of. You think they ought to be penalised because of that?'

'Of course not. But then—everybody's born with different talents and attributes, and I don't think anyone ought to be ashamed of being a brilliant swimmer, say, because other people can't swim as well as they can. If you take pride in what's yours, that doesn't imply that you're running down other people.'

'Maybe not.' Alex gave a slow, almost rueful smile. 'I guess you're lucky to have a family you're proud of.'

'I am, I know. And so are you. You come from one of the most distinguished families in the whole country. I should know, because it's been part of my job to research their history. The Gillons have produced famous admirals, generals, and even a cabinet minister or two.'

She expected him to agree, even hoped he would show a flash of family pride of his own. But he simply stared at her, until her voice faltered away under the intensity of his look.

'You say I don't know you yet, Laura,' he said quietly, 'and I'll admit it. But you know what's wrong with what you're saying? You think you know me. And you don't really know me at all.'

She couldn't understand what he was getting at. And she was still puzzling over his comment when he had paid the bill and they were walking out of the restaurant together.

They stepped outside into a calm, warm evening. A red sun still hung just above the horizon. The traffic on the freeway had subsided to a trickle, and the noise of the cars was almost drowned out by the chattering of the cicadas.

'Now, in this temperature,' Laura thought out loud, 'I could actually walk around a little.'

'Round here nobody walks,' Alex said with a short laugh. 'Early mornings they jog a couple of blocks, and the rest of the time they take their cars. What we could do, though, is drive up to the caverns and then walk over to see the bats.'

'The bats?'

'At sunset they all come out from the caverns. It's quite a sight.'

'I'm not sure I like bats.'

'They won't touch you.' He unlocked his car, and gestured to her to get in. For a moment she hesitated, wondering if it would be better to ask him to drive her back to the motel before they argued even more. But she couldn't think of a polite way of insisting, so instead she slid back into the low car seat.

Carlsbad was cavern town, she discovered when they drove through the downtown area. Everything—garages, bars, motels, restaurants—seemed to be named after the caverns.

'Is there nothing in this town but caverns?' she exclaimed in amazement.

'That's the main reason why it's grown up as it has.'

'But I'd never heard of the Carlsbad Caverns till I came over here! I know the brochures say they're incredible, but, for heaven's sake, they're only holes in the ground.'

Alex smiled. 'You won't say that when you've seen them.'

'Want to bet?' Laura had seen caves before, in England and France, and she felt sure that Carlsbad's stalactites and stalagmites would come as no surprise to her.

'Wouldn't be fair, I'd be sure to win. You won't be able to go down the caverns tonight, of course, you'll need to come back in the daytime. I'd take you myself but I'll be busy all week, and I'm going over to Phoenix on Friday. Any chance you'll still be around next weekend?'

'I doubt it, but I can always come on my own.'

'No need for that. Darlene will bring you, or Susie-Jo. I'll ask around.'

Laura was tempted to retort that he needn't go to the trouble, but she guessed that this, too, was a part of his normal routine with visitors, and she didn't insist.

Once out of town, they followed the signs to the caverns, joined an assortment of cars in a big car park, and then took a path signed to the caverns themselves. To Laura's surprise, a steady stream of people were already travelling down it. Obviously the bats themselves rated as a sizeable, if peculiar, tourist attraction.

'No need to go further,' Alex said eventually. 'We'll see fine from here. See, over there, the cavern entrance?'

Laura looked around. It was a desolate landscape of rocky soil interspersed with prickly pears and scrubby bushes. Not far away the entrance to the cavern gaped, a huge black hole.

'Nothing'll happen till sunset,' Alex said. 'Let's move off the path and find a place to wait.'

They did this, in silence. The last shreds of their earlier antagonism seemed to have evaporated, and Laura felt unexpectedly at ease in Alex's company. There was something surreal about the whole business of standing in the countryside of New Mexico waiting to watch a load of bats, and the silence fitted the scene so well that she found it almost strange when Alex started to talk to her. They chatted lightly for several minutes about the other attractions of the area, then he said, 'I still don't understand what exactly it is that you do for the Exonbys.'

'I suppose you'd call me a private secretary. I handle correspondence, pay bills, and generally deal with the estate administration. Lord Exonby used to do most of that himself, but he's bedridden now, and Lady Exonby doesn't like to handle the business side of things on her own.'

'I see. So you have an accounting qualification?'

'No, I don't. The work really isn't demanding enough to justify their employing a fully trained accountant. I can keep books on a day-to-day basis, and I turn to a firm of professional accountants when I need expert advice.'

'Same here. I can tell if I'm in the red or the black, but doing the sums ain't my style.' He gave a slow, wide smile, one that reminded her of Anthony's comment about how easily he had wormed his way out of lessons at school. 'So you're not a career girl?'

'Not really. I told you, I'll be getting married in a few months' time.'

'And you plan to throw up your job then?'

'Not immediately, no. I chose the job largely because I knew it would fit in well with living at Maltwood. It's not far to travel each day. I can vary my hours when I need to, and take holidays when Anthony chooses. We don't plan to do a great deal of entertaining, so I should be able to keep on working until I have children.'

Alex hesitated for a moment, then he said flatly, 'I guess so.'

Laura smiled. 'Really, I'm doing precisely what you criticised Englishmen for doing earlier, aren't I? My job isn't all in all to me, it's just one part of my life. I didn't choose it so I could build up a high-powered career or earn a fortune. Those aren't my priorities in life.'

'I'm not saying they should be,' Alex retorted. 'But if you're going to work at all, I'd have thought you'd go for something with a little more challenge to it.'

'Actually I find it fascinating working at Exonby. You might think the place is boring, but it isn't boring to me.'

'I didn't say it was. That wasn't what I meant. I used to find plenty to interest me in being a barman, I never got bored doing it. But jobs like that don't test you, don't stretch your abilities. I'd have thought you might go for something that did.'

'I'd say coming out here to track you down is stretching my abilities pretty well!' Laura said with a light laugh. It wasn't a proper answer to Alex's serious question, and she knew it, but she didn't want to answer him properly, not least because she knew he did have a point. Her work at Exonby rarely set her adrenalin flowing, but that was surely a small shortcoming in what was basically an enjoyable way of life.

'You've never done something like this before?'

'Good heavens, no! Nor am I likely to do anything like it ever again.'

'I guess not. It's just that—oh, I don't know, I'd have thought you'd ask for more from life than that. Marrying Downing, and a little job with the Exonbys. Just goes to show, I suppose, how little I know about you. I'd have taken you to be an A student, the kind of girl who'd go to college and get a degree.'

'Actually I did go to college.'

'To study what?'

'Law. I have an honours degree in law.'

'You have a law degree, and you mess around typing letters for Lady Exonby!'

'It's not a crime, you know!' Laura retorted with growing annoyance.

'No, but it's a damn waste. That's how the whole thing strikes me, as a waste. You're capable of more, you ought to be getting out there and looking for more.'

'Not everybody treats life like a poker game!'

'Nor do I! I don't say you have to raise the stakes till you go bust. But to settle at your age for a man like Downing, and——'

'That's what gets you, isn't it?'

'That's what?'

'You don't really care about my career, do you? This conversation isn't really about my job. That's what bugs you, that I'm going to marry Anthony Downing. You barely know the first thing about Anthony, it's twenty years since you met him, and yet you've fixed on this idea that he isn't man enough for me. Well, I can tell you, you're as wrong as can be!'

She glared at him, expecting him to argue back, or to deny vehemently that that was what he had been suggesting. But he simply shrugged and said, 'I didn't say that.'

No, but you thought it, Laura thought to herself. She was too annoyed to continue the conversation, and they fell back into silence.

I've certainly blown that, Laura thought sadly. I come over here to charm Alex Gillon and entice him back to Exonby, and instead I find myself scrapping with him from the very moment we meet! It hasn't been all my fault by a long way, but it's hardly what I intended to happen. It hasn't lost me much, though, because I can't see that I'd have had much hope of succeeding whatever I did or said. He isn't coming. That's as clear as it possibly can be.

And maybe, she continued to herself, that's the right thing to happen. Alex wouldn't fit in readily with

Gloucestershire society. His clothes, his manners, his attitudes, everything about him would seem alien back in Exonby. Even if it was what he wanted to do, it wouldn't be easy for him to reverse twenty years of growing away from England, and to turn back into a typical British aristocrat.

Twenty years? Perhaps it had been even more than that, for it didn't sound as if Alex at nineteen had been any better a fit with the Exonbys than he was now. His blunt, common sense, anti-intellectual approach to life; his soaring ambition; his impatience with fools and time-servers: none of those was a quality likely to endear him to his family and their acquaintances. It wasn't by chance that he had chosen to look elsewhere for a home. Here he fitted in far better than he ever could have done back in Gloucestershire.

Her task of bringing Alex Gillon back home had made such complete sense to her when Lord and Lady Exonby had suggested it, but now she wasn't at all sure that it would be the right thing to do.

But it's not for you to decide, Laura, she reminded herself. You're not here on holiday, you're working for the Exonbys, and you ought to carry on working in their interests until the minute you leave New Mexico. Remember that, and try to keep a little cooler!

'It's starting,' Alex said.

Laura pulled herself away from her thoughts, and looked up. The sun was just dipping below the horizon now, and the clear sky was stained a deep red. From the black hole of the cavern mouth, a small dark shape rose up, and away into the sky. Then another came, and another, and then so many that for a few minutes the entire sky was dark with tiny fluttering shapes.

Though she knew they were bats, if she hadn't been told that she would have taken them for small birds. They didn't come near; all she could see were black silhouettes. She didn't find them repulsive at all, but there was something eerie about the sheer size of the scene. In England it would have been unusual to see more than a couple of bats, but here there were hundreds, thousands, tens of thousands of them. There were more bats than she had thought possible.

It had the surreal grandeur of a horror film about it. Unconsciously she moved a step closer to Alex, and he put a reassuring arm around her shoulders. They watched together, in silence, as the vast cloud of bats rose up, and then slowly, slowly, dispersed into the rapidly darkening sky.

The crowd of watchers began to disperse too, moving in a chattering line up the path towards the car park. Laura became very conscious of Alex's arm around her. This wasn't what she'd had in mind, but she didn't want to antagonise him by drawing away too decisively, and, though she barely admitted it to herself, she wasn't at all sorry to be so close to him.

'Let's go,' he said softly. His hand slid down to capture hers, and they joined the procession together.

They didn't speak again until they were back in the car. Then Alex glanced across at her and said, 'Quite something, wasn't it?'

For a moment she found it hard to think what he was talking about. The bats weren't uppermost in her mind. But a little thought made it obvious, and she agreed, 'Yes, it was. Really astonishing.'

For just a moment, his eyes held hers, and she expected him to say something more. But he didn't, he just turned away, abruptly, and fumbled for the ignition key.

They drove back in silence. When he dropped her at the motel an hour later it was fully dark, and the stars were out in profusion.

'I won't come in,' he said. 'I've an early breakfast meeting tomorrow.'

I didn't ask you to come in! Laura thought irritably.
But all the same she hesitated to get out of the car. She
felt as if the encounter wasn't over yet, as if there was
still much more to be said and done.

'I maybe won't see you again before I go back to
England,' she said uncertainly.

'Maybe not. Tell the Exonbys—well, send them my
regards, you know. No hard feelings. But it wouldn't
solve anything for me to come back now.'

'In a way I understand that.'

'You do? Then there's hope for you yet!'

She gave an uneasy laugh, and Alex joined in too. But
it didn't break the tension between them; it seemed to
heighten it.

'Well—goodbye, Alex.'

'Goodbye, Laura. Take care.'

Laura knew she ought to go, but somehow she couldn't
bring herself to open the door and climb out. She almost
certainly wouldn't see him again for months or years;
she might never see him again. She needed these few
moments, to fix him in her memory. The stark, clear
lines of his face, his vital mane of hair, his eyes, almost
black in the darkness, his bright clothes—everything
about him suddenly mattered intensely to her.

There was a sort of inevitability about it when he
moved slowly forwards, and let his lips just brush across
her forehead.

Silence again. Then his hand caught her shoulder in
a firm grip, pulling her hard against him. His mouth
found hers and held it, not softly, but in a harsh, bruising
kiss.

Laura's world spun. The whirlwind that was Alex
Gillon had her caught and trapped, but only for a second,
before he was releasing her and she was subsiding,
breathless, against the car seat.

'I guess I shouldn't have done that,' Alex said, in a low, husky voice.

No, he shouldn't. And she shouldn't have responded as she had, with a sudden wild desperation, as if she was longing not only for his kiss, but for far, far more. Shaking, she turned away from him and fumbled for the door catch. She couldn't hear his car engine, and she was sure he was sitting there watching her as she hurried up the path to the hotel entrance, but she didn't let herself look back.

There was a phone call for Laura the following morning, when she was halfway through a huge breakfast of hash browns, fried egg and thin, crisp bacon. She took it in the hotel lobby, and found that it was from Susie-Jo Allen.

'I thought I'd catch you early,' Susie-Jo explained, 'before you rushed off sightseeing on your own. Alex said you'd like to see the caverns?'

'Yes—yes, I suppose I would.'

'I can make it this afternoon, if that'd suit you? Say I call for you at two? And then you must come back to our place afterwards for supper.'

'I'd love to, Susie-Jo. But are you sure I won't be putting you out? You must have seen the caverns before, surely?'

'Oh, dozens of times, but I always like an excuse to see them again. My mother looks after my daughter on Thursdays, so it's no trouble, honestly.'

'Then thanks—I'll look forward to it.'

Remembering the bats—and conscious of a few red patches where she had overdone her sunbathing the day before—Laura dressed in beige cotton trousers and a long-sleeved green T-shirt for the cavern trip. And, since she had found the path hard going in her high-heeled sandals the evening before, she swapped them this time for a pair of flat canvas shoes. A gaily patterned headscarf muted the effect of the blazing sun, and she was feeling quite like one of the locals when Susie-Jo pulled up outside the motel.

'No camera?'

'What a giveaway! Here was I, thinking I looked like an American tourist, and I'd never pass for one without a camera! Will I need one, though, going underground?'

'You can buy postcards if you'd rather, but you'll certainly want to come away with pictures of some kind.'

Laura wasn't convinced, and she assured Susie-Jo that she'd settle for cards.

But Alex's comments, and the phenomenal crowd of bats, should have warned her that she was in for something special! Carlsbad Caverns were on a scale that dwarfed her wildest imaginings. If the caverns she had seen before were tin huts, this was a positive Versailles! They passed from one huge space to another, gaping at stalactites the size of cathedrals, skyscraper stalagmites and rivers of crystalline rock. They walked through thrillingly small tunnels and along paths edged with precipitous drops. Nothing was garish or spoiled, but everything had been carefully planned for tourists, and the lighting effects were truly spectacular.

'Impressed?' Susie-Jo asked when they finally emerged from the cool of the caverns to the scalding heat of the outside world.

'Absolutely astonished,' Laura confessed.

'It always amazes me that the caverns aren't better known. Everybody who comes says they're more impressive even than the Grand Canyon.'

'I haven't seen that yet, but I can certainly believe it,' Laura said fervently. 'And to think the caves might stretch as far as the canyon itself...'

'Oh, yes, they go on for hundreds of miles. What we've seen is just the tiniest bit of them.'

'Well, that's more than enough to blow my mind!'

'Not absolutely, I hope.' Susie-Jo laughed. 'I've got lots more questions to ask you about England still!'

Unlike Alex, Susie-Jo liked to talk when she was driving, and Laura had already learned that she and Kent planned to make a trip to England the following year. 'I've lots more to tell you,' Laura responded, 'but I *was* hoping to ask a few questions myself.'

'About New Mexico?'

'More about Alex Gillon.'

'Ah-hah. Tell me first, though: who are these common friends you and Alex have in England?'

'I wouldn't really call them common friends,' Laura replied cautiously. 'We know some of the same people, but we've known them at very different times. Alex hasn't been in England since I was a small child, so I guess he's telling the truth when he says he barely remembers them. And he's certainly telling the truth when he says he belongs over here now.'

'Well, you sure did astonish us when you let it out that he was English! I'd always reckoned he came from Phoenix, Arizona.'

'He worked there for a while, he told me.'

'I guess so, but he's been here for a good ten years now. And boy, has he changed our little town! It used to be the sleepiest old place, but when Alex gets going he's like a tornado. Northways must employ close on five hundred people here now, and that's to say nothing of the restaurants, the shops... even the Marbury relies upon the trade he brings in. We didn't have a decent motel in town when he first came here.'

'His business seems to have grown very fast.'

'True, but carefully,' Susie-Jo replied. 'Kent always says—Kent's a banker, you know? So he sees a lot of this kind of thing—Kent says he's never seen a businessman as cool-headed as Alex Gillon before. He takes risks, sure, but he checks everything out before he jumps.'

'He doesn't strike me as a cautious man.'

'You wouldn't reckon so if you saw him stock-car racing! He and Kent used to go sky-diving too, though I talked Kent out of that after Marilu was born. But Alex is—he's wild, but careful wild, if you know what I mean. He never gets drunk, never makes a fool of himself with women, never loses more than a few dollars at poker. That man never really lets go of himself, that's what I think. He pushes hard, but there's always something there reining him in.'

'Perhaps that's so,' Laura said slowly.

'You know his folks back in England?'

'Not his parents, no. His father is dead.'

'Pity. I'd sure like to know what went on there. I guess they weren't happy.'

'Otherwise he wouldn't have emigrated?'

'Otherwise he would have gotten himself married, honey!' Susie-Jo gave a throaty chuckle. 'Men from happy families always do. While, as it is, every single woman in town's been throwing herself at Alex Gillon for the past ten years, and not one has he caught.'

'Not Darlene Dixon?'

'Absolutely not. Oh, he dates Darlene, but he dates a dozen girls. Darlene knows she's got no hope of pinning him down, though she keeps on trying when she's in between admirers. But you, now—you might stand a chance.'

'Me!' Laura exclaimed.

'I saw the way he was looking you over yesterday, honey. No wonder, you're real pretty in that cute English way of yours. And you're different, you know? You're English like he is, so you'd maybe understand him better.

You might sneak in underneath those defences he keeps up so high against the rest of us.'

Might she? Might she? For a moment, Laura couldn't resist a glow at the thought that Susie-Jo could be right. But common sense quickly prevailed.

'That's flattering of you, Susie-Jo,' she said brightly, 'but I'm already pinned down myself. I've been engaged since last Christmas, and I'll be getting married in a few months.'

'Hey, how stupid of me! I saw your ring, then I forgot all about it. Oh, I just love engagements. Tell me all about him.'

Laura talked of Anthony all the rest of the way back to the motel. But somehow, after Alex, she found it hard to make him sound exciting.

It's just the effect of New Mexico on me, she told herself. I seem to be a different person out here: brasher, braver, more aggressive. I don't act as I would at home, and I don't seem to think as I would at home, either. I'm disorientated. It must be a sort of mental jet lag that has given me this stupid obsession with Alex Gillon— that, and nervousness about my assignment. Once I'm back at Exonby I'll be overjoyed to see Anthony again, and to get on with making our wedding plans.

Susie-Jo came into the hotel with her, as Laura wanted to change her clothes before going on to supper.

'Oh, Lady Mallingham,' the receptionist said, 'there's a fax message for you from England. It came while you were out.'

Laura accepted the long white envelope in which the fax had been sealed, and turned it over curiously. She wasn't expecting the Exonbys to contact her. What could it be?

'A love-letter?' Susie-Jo asked.

'Hardly. I expect it's from my employers back in England.'

'Shall I leave you on your own to open it?'

'No, there's no need. I'm sure it's nothing special.' She ripped the envelope open, and pulled out the single sheet of paper.

She saw immediately from the heading that it was from the Exonbys' solicitor, Jeremy Flowerdew. The message was quite short. Lady Exonby had asked him to contact Laura, to tell her that Lord Exonby had died peacefully the previous night.

CHAPTER FIVE

'HONEY, you've gone all pale!' Susie-Jo exclaimed. 'Is it bad news?'

'Yes, it is. It's my employer, Lord Exonby. He died yesterday.'

'Oh, Laura. Honey, I'm so sorry. Look, let me buy you a drink of something. A cup of coffee, maybe.'

'There's no need. Well—yes, perhaps.'

Susie-Jo hustled her into the motel coffee shop, saw her seated, went off to the counter, and a few minutes later was back with two cups of strong black coffee.

'Thanks,' Laura said. 'It's all right, Susie-Jo, I'll be fine now. He was a very old man, and we'd been expecting it for some time. So it's not a tragedy, just a bit of a shock that it should happen now.'

'Sure is. Hey, I hope this doesn't mean you'll have to cut short your trip?'

'I imagine it does. The Exonbys don't have children, and I wouldn't want to leave Lady Exonby alone for the funeral. But—it's difficult to explain, Susie-Jo, but it changes a number of things.'

'It won't affect your job? I don't know how these English lordships work. Will his successor keep you on?'

Heaven knows what his successor will do, Laura thought, remembering Alex Gillon's stark prophecies of the previous morning. But she didn't feel she could explain all that to Susie-Jo Allen, so she just said carefully, 'I'm sure Lady Exonby will need me for a while yet, so that's not a problem. The difficulty is—well, there are arrangements to make. There'll be people to tell about the funeral service, perhaps a memorial service in London to organise, the details of the will to be sorted out, and so on.'

'People to tell? Hey, does Alex Gillon know these people, Lord and Lady whatsit? Ought you to tell him about it?'

'Yes. Yes, he does know them. And I suppose I must tell him.'

'Well, I shouldn't do anything right now, honey. It's always a shock when somebody you know well dies, even if you were expecting it. I'd take it gently this evening, then maybe you can chase Alex up over the weekend.'

'Maybe you're right.' Laura sipped at the coffee. It was scalding hot, and very strong. She couldn't help thinking of poor Lady Exonby, alone at the Hall. She hadn't only lost her husband, she would also lose the house that had been her home for half a century. And what would happen to it then?

Alex surely won't do anything too fast, she thought. He'll give Lady Exonby time to recover. He'll have to apply for permission for whatever he plans to do with the Hall. He'll surely have to come to England now. Maybe he'll come for the funeral. I really shouldn't put off telling him. He ought to know right away that he's now the Fourth Earl of Exonby.

'I think maybe I should contact Mr Gillon today,' she said slowly.

'I'm sure there's no need, Laura. He can't have seen these people for years, surely. It won't mean all that much to him, will it?'

'I don't suppose he'll be devastated, but all the same, he—look, it's difficult for me to explain, but there are reasons why he ought to know about it immediately.'

'Tell him tomorrow, then. Or would you rather call him up and tell him now?'

'I think I ought to tell him in person. Maybe... Oh, I just remembered. Tomorrow's Friday, isn't it? He said he was going off on a business trip on Friday.'

'Then I'll give him a call now, and see if we can drop over right away. It's on the way back to our place. You just drink your coffee, and I'll be back in no time.'

Susie-Jo had gone before Laura had had time to think about this suggestion, or to protest that this might not be the best way to break the news to Alex. It really did seem to her that it was important to tell Alex as soon as possible, but she would have preferred to do it while they were alone, and not with Susie-Jo Allen as an interested audience.

Still, he was a man used to keeping his thoughts and feelings to himself, and, as she had said to Susie-Jo, he would hardly be overwhelmed with grief at the death of an uncle he hadn't seen in twenty years. She would probably be able to tell him without either of them giving it away to Susie-Jo that he was the new Lord Exonby, and it seemed to her that that would be the best thing to do.

'He's at home, honey,' Susie-Jo said, settling back down on the coffee-shop bench. 'I said we'd call over for a cocktail in half an hour or so. I did ask him to join us for supper, but he's got some work to clear up before his trip, he said.'

Alex's house was about a mile out of town, down a long, quiet road lined with large, ranch-style properties. Laura was expecting something large and luxurious, and she wasn't disappointed. The drive wound through perfect green lawns, and up to a broad gravelled forecourt that gave on to three garages as well as the entrance to a big wooden house with a deep, overhanging veranda.

Alex himself was at the door to greet them by the time Susie-Jo's car scrunched to a halt on the gravel. He was dressed for the scalding weather, in pale green swimming-trunks and a matching green patterned shirt that he had left unbuttoned, showing off a great deal of tanned flesh. However hard he worked, he clearly found time to enjoy the sun—and to keep himself in good shape too, Laura noticed. His body was solid and muscular, without a spare inch of flab to be seen.

'Come out the back,' he said. 'I've fixed us some drinks by the pool.'

Laura had just a glimpse of large rooms either side of the hallway as they passed through the house. It was a modern house, with a great deal of exposed wood, and long pale shag carpets on the floors. Open shelves displayed a collection of silver, which Laura recognised as native Indian work, similar to some she had seen in an expensive souvenir shop downtown, and there were Indian hangings on the walls.

Behind the house, a garden awash in brightly flowering shrubs surrounded a patio which boasted a huge built-in barbecue and a circular swimming-pool. Alex led them over to where a tray with three glasses had been set on a table near the poolside.

'I thought Lady Laura ought to try a mint julep while she was down south,' he commented, handing them each a pale green drink. 'Or have you had one already?'

'No,' Laura said, 'it's my very first.' She took a long sip at the cool, strong, minty drink, in which the usual mountain of crushed ice was just beginning to dissolve in the blazing heat.

'Laura's had some sad news,' Susie-Jo told Alex, as she stretched out on a poolside lounger and set her drink down on the flagstones beside it.

'Oh?'

'Yes, a message came for me while we were out this afternoon. Lord Exonby died yesterday. Peacefully, in his sleep.'

Alex didn't react at all. Not a muscle moved in his hard-hewn face. Nor did he reply for a moment. Then he set down his drink and said quietly, 'I'm sorry. You must have known the old guy pretty well.'

'I did, yes. I've only been working for the Exonbys for a few months, but they were family friends, so I've known him all my life.'

'How has Lady Exonby taken it?'

'I really don't know yet. The message came to me through the family solicitor, but I'll have to phone her very soon. I hadn't thought—what time will it be in England?'

'Right now? Night time. You'd do better to call early morning.'

'Do you remember him, Alex?' Susie-Jo asked.

Alex swung round rapidly to confront her. Laura sensed his alarm, and said quickly, 'I told Susie-Jo that you'd known the Exonbys years ago. You won't re-member them well, I suppose.'

'Well enough to place them,' Alex said, with a sideways glance at her. 'I guess Lord Exonby was a decent guy in his way. He was getting old even before I came out here, though.'

'He was ninety-two.'

'Quite an age,' Susie-Jo said. 'But it's so weird, Alex, to think of you knowing lords and ladies in England. You've never said a word about it in all the time you've been here.'

'I never thought about it,' Alex said shortly. 'Hey, do you two want to take a dip while you're here? You could most likely do with one if you've been driving down to Carlsbad and back in this heat.'

It was a blatant attempt to change the subject, but that was no surprise to Laura. Naturally he would want to absorb the news before deciding what—if anything—he would tell his friends about his English inheritance.

'I'd love to,' she agreed. 'But I don't have a swimming costume with me, I'm afraid.'

'No sweat, Laura,' Susie-Jo said. 'I'm pretty sure I've a spare bikini with me in the car, and we must be the same size, near enough.'

'Well, if you're sure...'

'I'll go get it right now.'

Susie-Jo disappeared into the house, and Laura and Alex were left alone. Laura felt a moment's apprehension. What would Alex say now?

In fact he just said quietly, 'You'd better tell Lady Exonby I'll be in touch. And tell her I'm sorry to hear the news.'

'She'll expect you to—you know, send flowers and all that.'

'You imagine I wouldn't?'

She had thought it entirely possible that he wouldn't, but she didn't dare to say so. Then Susie-Jo reappeared, with a red bikini in one hand and a black one in the other, so there wasn't any opportunity for her to say anything more.

'You choose, honey,' Susie-Jo said cheerfully.

Laura took the black one, and Alex directed her to a room where she could change: a bedroom, large, and comfortably furnished in a blend of modern and traditional styles, with a complex patchwork quilt overlaying a modern divan.

Susie-Jo's spare bikini proved to be skimpier than those she normally wore, but it fitted her well once she had adjusted the shoulder-straps. She checked her appearance in the mirror. She looked strikingly pale in contrast to the two Americans, but her figure was good, and the black of the bikini emphasised the curves that her choice of dresses usually played down. Then she made her way back to the terrace, where Alex and Susie-Jo were already in the pool.

She stood for a moment, watching them. They were romping, rather than swimming seriously, but it was easy to see that they were both strong swimmers. With a pool of his own, Alex probably swam daily, and Susie-Jo and Kent most likely possessed one too. In England her family and friends were comparatively well off, but few of them had pools of their own—let alone this glorious sunshine to enjoy them in. To her it was a holiday, but this lifestyle was one that these people enjoyed all the time. Perhaps it wasn't such a wonder that Alex didn't feel any eagerness to return to rainy England.

Alex paused in his stroke, and turned to look at her. She saw his eyes narrow in the sunlight, and sensed his frank appreciation of what he saw. For a moment, she took a guilty pleasure in standing there, basking in his admiration. The memory came back, with alarming suddenness and strength, of his kiss the evening before.

Had she really known him for a bare two days? Even though she didn't feel she understood him, it felt as if he had always been a part of her life. She didn't want to bring him back to Exonby just in order to do her job properly, or to ease Lady Exonby's difficulties. She wanted him to be where she was.

Oh, no! She couldn't be falling in love with Alex Gillon. How could she, when she already loved Anthony and was engaged to marry him? To kiss another man even once had been bad enough, but it was a thousand times worse to be standing there wishing that it would happen again.

Thinking like that was dangerous. Alex Gillon was dangerous. Anyway, she and Alex were as different as two people could possibly be. There couldn't be any future for them, even if she weren't committed to another man. You're off balance, Laura, she told herself firmly. It's the heat, the news you've just received, the impact of that mint julep. Don't kid yourself that it's anything more than that, because it isn't, and can't be.

'Come on!' Susie-Jo shouted. 'The water's wonderful.'

Laura didn't hesitate any longer; she took a running dive into the water, and surfaced, dripping, a moment later. The water wasn't artificially heated, but the sun had taken the chill off it, and it was pleasantly cool rather than icy.

For a few moments they all swam around lazily, then Susie-Jo made for the side and reached out to retrieve her mint julep. 'Want yours, Laura?' she called.

'Not yet.' Laura dived under the surface, and stayed under for a little while, enjoying the enveloping coolness, and briefly glad to get away from the morass of questions that seemed to surround Alex Gillon.

She surfaced to hear a telephone ringing somewhere inside the house.

'I'd better answer it,' Alex said. He vaulted out of the water in a taut, easy movement, and loped across the flagstones towards the open door.

Laura watched him go. And Susie-Jo watched her.

'He's in pretty good shape, isn't he?' she murmured.

Laura glanced at her. She wasn't used to women commenting so approvingly on men's appearances, but she sensed that it was no more than the sort of casual comment Susie-Jo would make without a second thought.

'Yes, he looks to be.'

'I wish I could get Kent to work out every morning like Alex does. He'll get a real beer belly at the rate he's going.'

'I thought Kent was a very attractive man.'

'Oh, he's OK. But Alex ... well!'

'He'll hear you,' Laura warned, as Alex reappeared through the door.

'So what?'

'It's for you, Susie-Jo,' Alex called. 'Kent wants a word.'

'Better go and see what my lord and master has to say.'

Susie-Jo climbed, dripping, out of the pool, and Alex dived back in.

'You like swimming?' he called, surfacing towards the far side of the pool.

'Yes, I do.'

'Come on, catch me, then!'

He turned as he spoke, and made in a fast crawl for the side of the pool. Laura hesitated for a moment, then she pushed forward, and began to swim after him.

The pool was large enough for a serious game of tag, but small enough for Laura's slower speed not to be a crippling disadvantage. By the time Alex had reached the edge, tucked into a racing turn, and set off in a different direction, she was only a couple of arm-lengths from him. She swerved, trying to angle herself to cut off his path. But he saw her as he turned his head to breathe, and knifing his body, went into a sharp dive.

Under her, past her, and Laura, silently cursing him but enjoying the exhilaration at the same time, dived too. She could see the shadow and stir of him on the surface above her. She held herself under for a moment, planning where to intercept him, then pushed upwards.

If he was trying to evade her, he was too slow. Her hand scraped his foot. He hesitated, stopped, and slowly turned to confront her, treading water.

'Well caught. Now it's my turn. I'll give you five. One, two, three...'

Laura took a deep breath and was away. Straight towards the far edge, then curving as she sensed him begin his chase, then gulping another breath, and diving.

He let her zigzag across the pool for three or four minutes, always following her, but never catching, until her breath began to grow short, and she sensed that he was playing with her, giving her a decent run before moving in for the kill. She touched the side, turned, and changed tactics, making straight for him in a tidy crawl. He had to slow to a halt to change direction. But he saw her plan, and was round before she was a couple of feet beyond him. Panting and exhausted, she just made it to the edge before he reached her, stretching out a hand either side of her, and pinning her in place.

She wasn't quite finished yet. She breathed in again, and tried to slither down and past him. He was too quick for her, though. He caught her upper arm in a tight grip, and hauled her up against him.

Her breath left her, in a sudden surge of shock at the physical contact between them. From a short distance his presence had been powerful enough; at zero distance it was positively overwhelming. There was nowhere to go, nowhere to look but at him. His arm went round her, and her eyes came up, instinctively, to meet his fiercely narrowed gaze.

The water barely came halfway up their chests. The first cool touch of Alex's skin had faded already, and now she could feel the warmth of his sun-kissed body. His eyes had lightened in response to the bright light reflected on the water. Drops of water glistened in his hair, on his lashes, in the tawny mat of hair on his chest. Then his head came down to meet hers, and her eyes closed in anticipation of his kiss.

His lips were warm, their touch firm, strange and yet enticingly familiar. There was none of the arrogance, the forceful, demanding nature that she had seen so clearly in their earlier encounters. Instead she sensed an entirely unexpected gentleness and sensitivity within him.

She had been telling herself that he would never kiss her again, but now it seemed completely inevitable that he should. At some deeper level of her mind, she knew, she had been waiting all day for just this to happen.

Mindlessly, she opened her mouth under his, and brought her arms round his neck, straining her body to his and tangling her hands in the short hair at the back of his neck. Her nipples had hardened into sharp points of sensitivity, crushed against the broad expanse of his chest. His hands drifted downwards, moulding her body to his, and his lips and tongue moved restlessly, searching, questioning. But it wasn't a time for answers, or for thought at all. It was a world of heat and coolness, touch and taste and smell: a world of sheer sensation.

'Hey, you two, Laura and I ought to be on our way.' They didn't hear the soft pad of Susie-Jo's bare feet on the flagstones, and they barely took in her cheerful voice. 'Uh-oh,' Susie-Jo went on, quite unabashed, 'excuse me, folks. I guess I'd better see you back in the house.'

Slowly, Alex's mouth drew away from Laura's own; slowly he loosed his grip. She drifted backwards against the side of the pool, regained her footing on the smooth pool bottom, and began to take in with appalling clarity the fact that Susie-Jo had just seen her in Alex's arms.

'I guess I shouldn't have done that while you were off balance,' Alex said in a harsh-toned voice.

Laura didn't answer him. Her mind was whirling.

'Hell,' he went on, 'I've enough problems at the moment without finding you so damn irresistible. Look, we've got to talk, Laura, and not just about Exonby. We need to talk about us and get this whole thing straightened out.'

'But there isn't—I can't——'

'Don't tell me you're in love with Downing,' Alex went on inexorably, 'because I won't believe it. All right, I don't know him, and I don't know what goes on between the two of you, but I do know that you don't act to me like a woman who's in love with another man.'

'But, Alex, you don't understand, I——'

'Not now,' Alex interrupted. 'Susie-Jo's waiting, and that woman sure gets impatient if people don't pay her enough attention. I'll fix to see you another time soon.'

He vaulted on to the poolside, and reached out a hand to Laura. Awkwardly, she took it, and let him pull her up to join him. 'You'd better grab a towel,' he said, reaching out to a pile on one of the nearby chairs, and handing her one.

He waited till she was halfway towards the house, then he took a towel himself, and made in the same direction.

What on earth had come over her? Laura was shivering with fury as she rubbed herself down in Alex's luxurious spare bedroom. She wasn't the sort of woman who went about kissing strange men. Heavens, she hadn't so much as touched another man in the two years she had been seeing Anthony regularly. And then to respond so blatantly, to positively invite his embraces, when she had barely known him a couple of days, and was engaged to someone else!

It's the shock of hearing about Lord Exonby, she said to herself. But she knew even as she thought it that it wasn't true. The news had brought sadness, but no particular surprise. It wasn't a tragedy, and even if it had been that was no way to react to it. It wasn't the news that had made her react to Alex as she had done, it was the man himself, and the effect that he had on her now, and had had ever since the first moment she had seen him.

Alex Gillon is dangerous, she thought to herself. Dangerous and unpredictable—that's what Anthony called him. In every other way he's totally unlike the 'duffer' I'd expected to meet, but Anthony certainly was right about that! He's not a ladies' man in the super-ficial, charming sense, but when it comes to charisma and sheer raw sex appeal, God's hand must have slipped when He was doling out Alex Gillon's share.

She had been trying to protect herself by telling herself that every woman responded to him as she did, and that she meant nothing special to him, but it was painfully clear now that that wasn't true. What would he say to her when they talked? He would ask her to end her en-gagement, she supposed—but what would he offer her to put in its place? And what would she say in return?

She really didn't know. All she knew was that she truly was disorientated and overwrought, and that this couldn't be the right time for her to make major de-cisions about her life. She needed to get back to England, to the familiar, reassuring surroundings of Exonby, and then, surely, she would see things in a clearer light.

Thank heavens he was leaving town the following day. She didn't believe he'd cancel his business trip because of the news, and she knew she would have to leave New Mexico as soon as possible—before his return. So if Alex did want to talk to her at length, he would have to come to England to do it.

He'd have to come to England in any event, wouldn't he? She didn't dare to take it for granted that he would. But if he did, then they would be talking on her territory, not on his. If he did, he'd surely see that his future as well as hers lay in England, at Exonby. And if he didn't—well, perhaps when she got back to England she'd realise that these alarming new feelings were all a mirage, and that really her love for Anthony was as strong as ever.

She zipped up her trousers, slipped her T-shirt over her head, and a moment later she had tracked down Susie-Jo and Alex in a big, low-ceilinged living-room, where they were standing uneasily together, clearly waiting for her.

Alex saw them out to Susie-Jo's car.

'I'll be away till next Wednesday,' he said, leaning over the open door as Laura got into the passenger seat. 'But I'll be in touch with you as soon as I get back.'

'You'll know where to find me.'

'Sure do.' He reached across and just touched the back of her hand, then turned and strode away.

Laura watched him go. You were thinking of the Marbury Motel, she thought to herself, and we won't be meeting there. But I told the truth, because you will know where to find me. I'll be at Exonby.

Laura wasn't alone with the Allens for supper. Susie-Jo's mother had returned their small daughter Marilu, and a couple of neighbours were there too. They ate barbecued steak and hamburgers in the back yard, around a pool almost as large as Alex's, and Laura, now feeling a reaction to the traumatic events of the day, gratefully accepted the large Scotch that Kent offered her.

It didn't taste strong, served up with crushed ice, but by the time her glass had been refilled twice she was beginning to feel a little hazy—full, tired, and not nearly so anxious to worry over things that she couldn't change.

She didn't raise the subject of Alex Gillon, but she knew it was all but inevitable that somebody would mention him, so it was no surprise when Kent Allen finally said to her, 'Susie-Jo said Alex knew your boss pretty well when he was in England?'

'I suppose he did.'

'Then I reckon his own family must be pretty high up in English society?'

'That doesn't follow. Most people in England must know a few members of the aristocracy.'

'I never met nobody before who did.'

'Perhaps you don't know all that many English people, Mr Allen.'

'I've met more than a few in my time,' Kent Allen replied. He didn't speak rudely, but he did speak with a solid conviction that told Laura she wouldn't be able to escape from the subject quite so easily.

'So how come Alex knows your boss, Laura?' Susie-Jo broke in.

'His family were—connections of the Exonbys.'

'Connections?' Kent picked up the word instantly. 'You mean relations?'

'Well—yes.'

'What sort of relations? Close relations?'

Laura flushed. She knew that Alex would be furious if he knew of this conversation. She guessed that, even now he had actually inherited the earldom, he would choose not to mention it to his neighbours. But she didn't want to offend Kent—or Susie-Jo—by refusing to answer.

Anyway, she thought to herself, why *should* Alex be so prickly about the whole business? It was no disgrace to be the Earl of Exonby—far from it. He should have been proud of his family and their position in society.

And he should—he absolutely *must*—come back to England. She wasn't at all sure that the joint lure of herself and Exonby would bring him there. So it had to be a good thing, didn't it, to enlist his friends in support of her cause?

She couldn't see any good reasons for keeping Alex's inheritance secret—except the fact that he had made it clear that that was what he wanted. While there were, now she stopped to think about it, several reasons for telling Kent Allen what he wanted to know.

'Actually,' she said, 'Alex is Lord Exonby's nephew.'

'His nephew!'

'That's right. He's the son of Lord Exonby's younger brother.'

There was silence for a moment, while everybody absorbed this information, then a buzz of conversation began to mount up all around the poolside.

'Hang on,' Susie-Jo said. 'Let me get this straight. Alex is Lord Exonby's brother's son? So how come his name isn't Exonby too? Or did he change it?'

'No, he didn't change it. Gillon is the family surname, you see. Exonby is just the name of their earldom.'

'So Lord Exonby's name was Gillon too?'

'That's right. He was George Frederick Gillon, Third Earl of Exonby, Baron Gillon of Brownswood, and Viscount Duckenham.'

'What a mouthful!'

'It is rather.' Laura took a big gulp of whisky, to boost up her confidence before carrying on with the rest of her revelation. 'I suppose it's no wonder really that Alex has a few qualms about taking it all on board.'

'On board?' Susie-Jo echoed. 'Laura, what do you mean?'

'The title's all his now. The late Lord Exonby didn't have a son, you see, so it passes from him to his brother, Alex's father, who died before him, and from Alex's father to Alex himself. So, as of yesterday, Alex Gillon is the Fourth Earl of Exonby.'

'Holy Moses!'

The dead silence that followed this was rather pleasing to Laura. Even the impervious Alex Gillon would be a little shaken if he were there to witness it, she decided. What a pity he wasn't! Or rather, what a relief, because now she could press on with putting her case without his preventing her, as he doubtless would have done if he had been there.

'It's a very distinguished title,' she said with slightly drunken solemnity. 'Queen Victoria bestowed it on the

First Earl more than a hundred years ago. It entitles Alex to sit in the House of Lords, of course. And he automatically inherits the family estate too. There's a Queen Anne mansion in Gloucestershire, with seventy rooms, and a deerpark, and a substantial amount of farmland as well.'

'Laura,' Susie-Jo said, 'did Alex know this was going to happen? Before you came?'

'Of course he did. He's known since he was a boy that he would inherit when his uncle and his father died.'

'And he never breathed a word!'

'I guess this means we'll all have to curtsy to him now,' the Allens' neighbour, Myra Bentsen said, laughing. 'Call him your lordship. Is that right, Lady Laura?'

'Your Grace, isn't it?' Kent asked.

'Oh, no,' Laura said, with an angry look at Myra Bentsen. This wasn't funny, she thought hazily. It was a very serious business, getting people's titles right. People shouldn't laugh at these time-honoured rules. 'Only dukes get called your Grace. Your lordship is right for earls.'

'Alex'll never live this down,' Susie-Jo said with a giggle.

'He won't have to, honey. He'll clear off back to England, I guess.'

'He sure can't do that,' Bill Bentsen retorted. 'This town would never be the same without him. He's got a good team under him, true, but it takes a man like Gillon to keep an outfit like Northways growing all the time.'

'He must come back to England,' Laura said. 'At least for a while. Exonby is his inheritance, and he has to attend to it properly. Anyway, there have been Gillons at Exonby for centuries, so everybody's hoping that Alex will come back to live there permanently.'

'Your friends back in England may be hoping that, Laura, but we sure ain't hoping it round here,' Kent said strongly. 'Bill's right. This town can't do without him.'

'I don't know about that,' Laura said. She was beginning to feel a little uneasy. She had meant these people to be impressed when she told them of Alex's title, but that wasn't the word for their reaction. They were more surprised and intrigued, as if the whole thing was rather a joke.

But it was no laughing matter whether Alex decided to return to England or not. It was vitally important, not only to these people around her, but to Lady Exonby and to all the servants and tenants on the estate.

She wished she had drunk a little less and didn't feel quite so dopey, so that she could put her case with more conviction and determination. She did her best to explain to the Allens and the Bentsens why they should try to persuade Alex to return to England, but it seemed that, the more she said, the more she convinced them that it was essential that he remain in New Mexico.

After all, Susie-Jo said, if he were to see Exonby he might actually like it, and they couldn't afford to have him decide to stay there for good. England might be the home of centuries-old traditions, but New Mexico was a new, young state, still growing, and it needed Alex Gillon to help it grow.

Laura talked on and on, but she seemed to be going more and more round in circles. Finally Kent Allen got to his feet and said, 'Laura honey, you've had one hell of a day. I'm going to get you back to your motel, and make sure you have a good long sleep before you set about all this phoning and sorting out in the morning.'

CHAPTER SIX

LAURA woke next morning with a crashing headache, made all the worse by the sun that streamed through her window. The day seemed even hotter than the one before, though that was barely imaginable. She went down to the coffee shop for a quick breakfast, and collected a letter that had been left at Reception for her.

A single glance at the envelope told her who it was from—that arrogant, barely legible scrawl could only belong to Alex Gillon. She opened it when she got back to her room. The note inside was on Northways paper, extremely short, and even less legible than the envelope. No wonder Alex didn't normally write his letters by hand, Laura thought, as she struggled to decipher it. He was clearly no handier with a pen now than he had been in his schooldays.

> 'Dear Laura,
> If you need me, phone me at Northways in Phoenix. The number's above. I'll be back by five p.m. Wednesday. I'll pick you up at six for supper. Don't tell anyone about my inheritance.
>
> Alex.'

It was a little late for the last request, Laura thought wearily. Instruction, rather. Alex hadn't bothered to add a 'please', she noticed—and he had assumed that she would have supper with him, rather than inviting her.

Well, she couldn't. She'd be home in England long before Wednesday. She threw the note on to the unmade bed and picked up the telephone. Five minutes later, her plans confirmed, she was down at Reception finalising her booking on a plane from Albuquerque to Washington that evening, and another from Washington to London first thing the next morning.

Lord Exonby's funeral was held on a fine, clear day. The sun shone down—not with the force of the sun in New Mexico, but strongly by English standards—on the heap of roses that covered his coffin, and on the row of wreaths sent by all the friends he had made during his long life.

Laura was kept busy supporting Lady Exonby during the service, and only after they emerged from Exonby Church did she have a chance to meet the other mourners. Anthony was there, and his mother, her own parents, several dozen of the Exonbys' Gloucestershire neighbours, all the servants from the Hall, and the tenants of the farms on the estate. Almost all the faces were familiar to her, but she didn't recognise a middle-aged lady in a rather dowdy grey coat, or the stout, balding man at her side, or the smartly dressed younger woman who was perhaps their daughter. They were standing on the edge of the crowd of black-dressed figures, looking a little out of place as if they knew nobody else.

'Good heavens,' Lady Exonby whispered, 'I haven't seen Maud Gillon in thirty years.'

'Maud Gillon?'

'Over there in the grey. I can't remember her new name. And that must be Fenella. Haven't seen her since she was a child either.'

Maud Gillon! That was Alex's mother, Sandy Gillon's much younger wife, and Fenella was his sister. Laura knew their new names perfectly well, since she had written to them both shortly before leaving for New Mexico.

'Maud's now Mrs Eyre, and Fenella is Mrs Mitchell.'

'How extraordinary of them to come. I'll have to say something to them. You'll come with me, Laura? Then I can leave them with you to talk about New Mexico.'

Curiosity and embarrassment mingled in Laura, but Lady Exonby was already heading for the little group, so she had no option but to follow. A moment later Maud was introducing her second husband, Peter Eyre, a market gardener, and Fenella was explaining that her husband hadn't been able to take time off work to come to the funeral.

'He runs a shop, doesn't he?' Laura asked pleasantly.

'A shop? Good heavens, no. What made you think that? No, James is an accountant.'

It was a forgivable slip, but an embarrassing one, and it made Laura feel even less at ease. Lady Exonby too appeared edgy; she stayed only to receive their condolences before moving on to greet some other mourners.

'I told you we shouldn't have come,' Peter Eyre said to his wife as soon as Lady Exonby was out of earshot.

'Lady Exonby was ever so pleased to see you here,' Laura said awkwardly. 'I'm afraid she's in no frame of mind to chat today, but——'

'It's not that, miss. I said to Maud, they're not our kind of people, never have been and never will be.'

'I know, lovey, but we had to come. You see, miss,' Maud Eyre continued, turning from her husband to Laura, 'his lordship was good to me in the old days, and his father before him. And Fenella's one of the family, and——'

'And so are you, Mrs Eyre,' Laura hastily assured her.

'And it's got nothing to do with Alex,' Mrs Eyre went on vehemently. 'That's what my husband thinks, you see, that it's, like, Alex's family moving in on Exonby now that he's inherited. But Alex doesn't have anything to do with us any more, and we have nothing to do with him.'

'I know you haven't been in close contact recently, but now that he *has* inherited——' returned Laura hopefully.

'He hasn't come here, has he?' Fenella interrupted.

'We told you he wouldn't,' her mother said grumpily. 'Didn't I say to you, Fenella, us coming here today has got nothing to do with Alex? I said, we aren't going to hear from Alex ever again, even if he is his high-and-mighty lordship now.'

'I do hope you will,' Laura said nervously. 'I've seen Alex—that is, his lordship—myself very recently, and I'd be happy to pass on a message, or...'

To her surprise, both Fenella and her mother shook their heads. 'That's nice of you, miss,' Mrs Eyre said, 'but, like I said, we didn't come here today because of Alex, and we don't reckon to be coming back ever again.'

'I do hope you'll feel you can. Come back again.'

'Well, thank you, miss.' Mrs Eyre narrowed her eyes, in a gesture oddly reminiscent of her son, and then said, 'Now don't you go making a tragedy out of it. We never were a close family and we just went in different ways, us and Alex, us and the Gillons. No hard feelings, that's just the way it is.'

'But now that Alex is the earl, if he ever does come over to Exonby...'

'Then he knows where to find us if he wants to,' Mr Eyre said brusquely. 'Not that we reckon he will. Come on, Maud, we should be on our way.'

'Oh, no!' Laura exclaimed. 'Everybody's going back up to the Hall now, for the funeral breakfast. You'll join us, of course, and...'

Her voice trailed away, as the three people in front of her all silently shook their heads.

'That's kind of you, Lady Laura,' Fenella said coolly, 'but we'd rather not. It's a long drive, nearly a hundred miles, you know, and we'd prefer to be pushing off.'

Laura didn't insist. She guessed that Alex's mother and sister shared his strength of mind, and that they wouldn't easily be persuaded. But that was all they did seem to share with him, she thought, bemused as she watched the family set off towards a slightly battered station-wagon. She couldn't see much of a physical resemblance to Alex in either of these pleasant-looking but unremarkable women, and they certainly didn't have his powerful presence, or his air of brash self-confidence.

'Who on earth were those people?' She swung round, and saw that Anthony had come over to join her.

'The new earl's mother and stepfather and sister.'

'Good heavens! Invading in force!'

'Hardly,' Laura said coldly. 'As far as I could gather they haven't been in contact with his lordship at all. And they only came to the service; they're not coming up to the Hall with us.'

'Looks like Gillon himself didn't even do that.'

'I suppose you'd take it to be *invading* if he had!'

'Laura! I don't know what's got into you since you came back from America. You seem to snap at me the whole time.'

'I'm sorry,' Laura said hastily.

'I know, darling, it's been a strain. But don't worry, it's almost over now.'

Yes, thought Laura silently, it is. Over. Alex hasn't attended the funeral, or even phoned or written. He's sent a wreath, and that's it. He'll do just what he threatened to do, sort out the business side of things from New Mexico, and never come here at all. I won't see him again. He hasn't changed his mind about Exonby, and as for me—well, he must have taken offence at my leaving without talking to him, or told himself he'd do better not to come between me and Anthony. It's finished before it even really began.

And here am I, still engaged to Anthony, with everybody around me thinking nothing has changed. Perhaps it hasn't. Perhaps in a few weeks Alex really will come to seem like something that happened in a strange dream, and I'll manage to feel for Anthony again what I felt for him before. And if I know now what I didn't know before—that another man can make me feel a desire I've never, ever felt for Anthony—then perhaps it will be as well to keep that as my secret, and to work on forgetting it as fast as I can.

She soon busied herself seeing a selection of elderly relations into limousines, and ten minutes later she had joined Anthony and his mother in the little procession of cars making the two-mile journey back to the Hall.

'How thoughtless,' Anthony said, as his Range Rover crunched over the gravel of the Hall drive, and round to the stables where all the cars were to be parked after the funeral. 'Some idiot has left his car right in front of the main entrance.'

'It's strange,' Laura agreed. 'I wouldn't have thought anyone could miss the ushers showing them where to go. Maybe it's one of the temporary staff, Anthony. We've hired nearly a dozen, since the house is full with relatives staying overnight.'

'Maybe so.' Anthony climbed out, slammed his door, and strode round to Laura's side of the car to help her out with his usual automatic courtesy. 'Did you manage to have a word with Lord Fanshawe?'

'Not that I recall. Remind me, who was he?'

The three of them talked, quietly, of the other mourners until they were joined by other people making their way through the great main door, rarely used but opened for this special occasion, and into the Rose Room where the funeral breakfast was to be held.

Since Laura had been held back ensuring that everybody had a lift back to the Hall from the church, the room was already crowded. Three or four hired waitresses, in black dresses with frilly white aprons, were circulating with trays of sherry. The tenants and the estate staff were standing in nervous groups, talking in low voices to each other. Lady Exonby was sitting in a high-backed chair by the window, with the Lord Lieutenant of Gloucestershire leaning over her.

And at the far end of the room, tall and severe in a well-cut dark suit and black tie, was the unmistakable figure of Alex Gillon.

Laura stopped so abruptly that Lady Downing walked straight into her, and the little commotion that this caused took her eyes from him for a minute. It's a dream, she told herself; a mirage. Of course Alex Gillon isn't here. Then she nerved herself to look up again, and she knew that he was only too real. Her heart seemed to leap into her throat and stay there. He came! she thought with sudden exultancy. He came, after all!

He was standing talking to a man whom Laura recognised as the Lord Fanshawe Anthony had just mentioned, a large landowner with an estate adjoining Exonby. Alex had a glass of sherry in his hand, he looked perfectly at home amid the architectural splendour of the Rose Room, and if Laura hadn't seen him looking equally at home in swimming-trunks in New Mexico she could have taken him for a typical English aristocrat. Only his deep tan betrayed his foreignness.

He didn't look her way.

'Who's the tall man with Fanshawe?' Anthony whispered.

Laura took a deep breath. 'That,' she said steadily, 'is the new Earl of Exonby.'

* * *

'Well, my dear,' Lady Exonby said, as the mourners were moving aside to collect their sandwiches and salad, 'so he came after all.'

'So he did.'

'I felt sure he would, though I must admit I had a moment of doubt when I didn't see him at the church. I knew you'd have done a good job of persuading him, even if you did try to warn me that you weren't certain you'd succeeded.'

Laura wasn't certain she'd succeeded! For the previous three days she'd been doing her utmost to bring it home to Lady Exonby that she'd failed! And the awful thing, the thing she couldn't explain here and now, was that she was afraid she might really have failed, whatever it looked like to the other woman. Had Alex Gillon really come to England because of Exonby, or had he come because of her? Or might he, just possibly, have come for a mixture of both reasons? She still didn't know.

'It's a great pity he wasn't at the service,' she said, in a rather desperate attempt to head Lady Exonby away from this unaskable, unanswerable question.

'That was most unfortunate. Apparently his flight was delayed. And one might have expected him to telephone or write to warn us he was coming.'

'He's a—difficult—man to deal with.'

'I can certainly believe that,' Lady Exonby said crisply. She looked over to where Alex Gillon was standing, empty glass in hand, staring out of the window. A steady succession of people had introduced themselves to him, but he had greeted them all brusquely, and ended the conversations almost immediately. Now word had evidently spread that the new earl was a touchy American who was best left alone, because nobody was making any attempt to talk to him.

'But we shall be charming to him just the same,' Lady Exonby went on. 'Ah, Mrs Tenbury-Smythe, how good of you to come.' She moved her head to look over Laura's shoulder, and Laura, knowing that she was dismissed, politely nodded to Mrs Tenbury-Smythe and moved away.

In the half-hour they had been in the room together, Alex had said not a word to her. He hadn't even looked her way when she was looking his. He had ignored her so totally that she guessed he was trying to force her into making the first move. And she ought to go up to him, she knew, and make some kind of apology for leaving New Mexico without responding in any way to his note, but she just couldn't bring herself to do it with Anthony and Lady Downing watching her.

As she watched, Anthony approached him. She saw Alex half turn, his face set granite-hard in an expression of cool disinterest, as Anthony introduced himself.

Alex was several inches the taller. His dark suit followed the taut lines of his body with expensive perfection; against it, Anthony's suit, which Laura knew to be several years old, looked faded and lumpen. Anthony always gave off an air of solid self-confidence, but Alex's self-contained aura of authority seemed to reduce the other man, like everybody else in the room, to the status of an insignificant minion.

It was acutely uncomfortable to her to see the two of them together. I'm going to marry Anthony, she told herself. Alex Gillon means nothing to me. But every tremor of her body seemed to give that statement the lie.

She watched the two of them for a moment more, then she abruptly turned and walked out of the Rose Room, and into the main hallway. There was a narrow passage to the left, leading to a small downstairs cloakroom, and she went along this, hoping to seize a moment's peace.

The cloakroom was mercifully empty, and Laura shut herself in the cubicle and set her forehead against the cool plaster of the outside wall. What now? she thought wearily. What on earth is Alex going to do now?

She stayed there alone for several minutes. Then, just as she was beginning to think that she ought to return to the Rose Room in case Lady Exonby needed her, she heard the sounds of the outer cloakroom door opening, footsteps, and women's voices.

'You must admit, though, it's a lovely suit he's got on. Doesn't look foreign, does it? I bet it came from Saville Row.'

That was the voice of one of the cleaners at the Hall; Laura recognised it immediately. And it was another cleaner who answered her, in the cheerfully complaining tone of a woman who nagged so often that she forgot she did it, 'He's rich, they say.'

'He'll need to be, to keep this place up.'

'But did you see his mother at the service? That terrible coat of hers! Now that was a Marks and Sparks job if you ask me.'

'Woolworths, more like. But, of course, there was never any money on her side of the family.'

'You were here back then, weren't you? When she was married to old Lordy's brother?'

'Oooh, she's gone downhill since those days. She wasn't smart when she came here, mind. Course, I was here back before she married old Sandy, when she was working here. Maud Higgins from Cirencester, that was her. She did the third-floor bedrooms when I did the second. None too handy with the hospital corners, but she knew how to flutter her eyelashes at old Sandy. And, of course, we all knew what old Sandy was like.'

'One for the girls, was he?'

'Different one every time he came. Sometimes two of them, one for each arm. He'd run after all of us maids if we didn't watch out, but we knew what he was after—least of all, most of us did.'

'Not Maud.'

'Well, my dear, I'd never have believed he'd marry her, not even when she found out she was in the family way. It had happened before, you know, a girl called Ruthie a couple of years earlier, and she got paid off and slipped out the back door sharpish. But Maud managed it somehow. Three months before the baby was born she got him to make it legal.'

'Good for her.'

'Wasn't really,' the other cleaner said sharply. 'Out of place, she was. The family never took to her. The last earl, and his father too, the second earl, they were always polite, but Lady Exonby would snipe at her something terrible. Old Sandy used to come here, and bring little Alex and his sister, but she soon stopped coming with them. Then we heard rumours the marriage was in trouble, and they must have been divorced before Alex was more than six or seven.'

'Just goes to show, doesn't it?'

'Doesn't it just? Mind, to think that Maud Higgins' boy is the earl now!'

'Oh, but he takes after his uncle, don't you think? He's the image of old Lordy when he was a few years younger.'

'In looks, maybe, but there's a lot of Maud in him, you mark my words. You know he got expelled from Darlingforth? Never heard what he did, mind, but the rumours that flew about then! It was worse than old Sandy's day. Sandy, he was a ne'er-do-well, but there was nothing sly about him, nothing clever, you know? It was Maud that had all the cunning. Well, she had to have, didn't she, to get him to marry her?'

'And they say he's made a fortune, out in California or somewhere...'

'Oil prospecting, wasn't it . . .?'

This last Laura heard only faintly, for the two women, their make-up doubtless repaired and their hair combed, were leaving the cloakroom as they said it. Then there was silence. She kept standing in the cubicle for several minutes longer, as her thoughts fell into place. Then she slowly unlocked the door, gave a bare glance at her pale face in the mirror, and made her way back to the Rose Room.

Alex Gillon was walking out of the door just as she reached it. Her heart felt as if it had stopped, and she thought wildly of backing into the corridor again, but he had already seen her, so it was too late to try to escape.

'Laura,' Alex said, in a harsh, uneven voice.

'Good afternoon, your lordship.'

'Oh, for heaven's sake, I can't stand for being called your lordship!'

But you're going to have to stand for it now, Laura thought suddenly to herself. Whether you like it or not, Maud Higgins' little boy is the Fourth Earl of Exonby now. And, not least for your *mother's* sake, Alex Gillon, I'm going to do everything I can to make sure that you play your part to the hilt. You can't run from the curious looks now, you can't hide in anonymity. Everyone here knows who you are. You're the Earl of Exonby, and that's what you will be for the rest of your life.

'In a couple of weeks, I expect you won't even notice.'

'I reckon I shall.' Alex took a step backwards, and leaned against the wall, just next to the doorway. He fixed Laura with a hard brown stare.

'It was dumb of me to write you that note,' he said abruptly. 'I should have known you'd have to go straight back.'

Laura's stomach sank, leaving a hollow, sick feeling behind it. Whatever there was, whatever there might be between them, he surely didn't plan to discuss it right then!

'Yes, I did have to,' she said nervously. 'I got the first flight.'

'And you think I should have done the same.'

'I—it might have been better. I know you didn't mean to miss the service, but... Still, I'm glad you finally came.'

'Are you?'

'Yes!' she hurled back.

She was thinking of Maud Higgins when she said it, and it was only a split second afterwards that she realised that he wasn't. He was thinking of her. And she'd given him an answer that she hadn't meant to give him, to a question that she hadn't yet heard—an answer that wasn't even strictly accurate, because she could still think of several reasons why it might have been better for them both if he hadn't come to Exonby. But it was said now. And she saw a flare of warmth in his eyes in recognition of it, then he seemed to sense that she was mentally withdrawing from him, regretting her reply, and his manner too suddenly cooled.

'Then you'd better fix me a hotel for tonight.'

'A hotel? But, your lordship, you'll stay here!'

Alex's brows lowered. 'Lady Laura,' he said in a cold, deliberate voice, 'I will not be called "your lordship" by you or by anybody else. My name is Gillon, Alex Gillon, just the same as it has always been. And I will not stay in this mausoleum of a house, I will stay in the nearest decent hotel that has a room with a bath free. Now, can you fix that for me, or do I have to find a phone for myself?'

'You can't,' Laura said bleakly. 'It won't do at all. Lady Exonby would have a fit. Think how it would look to everyone. This is your house now. You have to stay here.'

'Do I?'

Laura quailed at the expression in his eyes. It seemed obvious to her that it would be grossly insulting to Lady Exonby if he stayed in a hotel room, but it clearly wasn't to him. He'd never yet agreed to do anything because she thought it was the right thing to do, and it didn't look as if he was about to start now! She kept on making the same mistake, kidding herself she'd have a chance of manoeuvring him into doing what she wanted, when in reality this man was about as manoeuvrable as a ten-ton lorry!

'I really do think you do,' she said uncertainly.

'And I disagree. Nobody'll read it the way you think, not if you and I handle it right.'

You and I! Why's it got to be *my* job? Laura inwardly complained. But she knew why. Because he wanted it to be, and so did she; because he couldn't walk back into the Rose Room and ask anyone else, and she didn't dare to argue any longer, with just a thin wall between him and Lady Exonby, and much bigger battles still to come.

'The study's down this corridor.'

'Then let's go there.'

She led the way, very conscious of his heavy tread just behind her, and conscious, too, of the fact that he was arranging things so that they would, at least briefly, be alone together.

Alex shut the study door behind them, and Laura turned to face him.

'You know why I came,' he said in a low voice.

'Of course I do,' she shot back. 'I spent long enough trying to persuade you to do just that.'

His expression changed, again just momentarily, and she glimpsed—a strong emotion, sensed too briefly for her to be sure she'd identified it correctly. Then it was gone, and his face was as blankly uninformative as ever.

'How true,' he said. 'So who allocates the rooms to visitors here?'

'Mason. The butler—Lady Exonby's butler. Or rather, your butler. Your lordship.'

His lips thinned, and for a second she expected him to punish her for that, but he wasn't prepared to be distracted. 'Then you can tell Mason, from me, that as I arrived so late and unexpectedly I thought it would cause least inconvenience to Lady Exonby and her guests if I stayed elsewhere. If you tell it smoothly, he'll believe you without a second thought. But if you sense that he doesn't, then you tell him to make damn sure that everybody else he talks to believes *him* when he tells the same story. Right?'

Laura slowly shook his head. 'Mason can do that, he's very professional, but I still think you're making a mistake, Alex. Lady Exonby simply won't agree to your staying anywhere but here. The other guests may not know, but *she* knows that the Blue Room is empty and waiting for you.'

'You surely don't imagine I came here because I give a damn what Lady Exonby thinks.'

'Perhaps you think you don't, but you're mistaken, Alex. You don't really want to upset her, do you? She's your *aunt*, remember, and an elderly lady who's just been widowed. She's finding it just as difficult dealing with you as you find it dealing with her. If she can be gracious and welcoming, can't you make some effort to meet her halfway?'

'Not by staying here. I don't want you or her imagining you've won me round to taking on this place. That'll only store up more problems for the future. I haven't changed my mind on Exonby and I won't change it. That isn't why I came here, as you know damn well!'

'I can't see why else you should have come!'

'Can't you? Then let me remind you of the reason.'

She had thought she was alert to him now, had thought he couldn't take her by surprise. But the hands that came down on her shoulders and dragged her to him found her with no defence, no plan of escape. She barely had time to let out a little yelp of mingled astonishment and objection, to set her hands against the broad expanse of his chest and push ineffectually at it, before she was trapped tightly against him in the firmest embrace she had ever known.

His mouth didn't ask, didn't question; it took. With barely suppressed anger at first, and with bruising power. Then, as the resistance slid out of her body, and her lips slowly opened under the irresistible pressure of his, with a sweetness of honeyed intensity.

Laura's response was a trickle at first, a strange, unfamiliar tingling deep inside her, but it suddenly grew into a flood. Her hands eased around him, and strained against his back, pulling him closer and closer, though already there was not a paper's breadth between their two bodies. Her tongue found his, thrusting and exploring, and joined it in a strange savage dance of desire. This was what she had wanted, what she had sensed from the first moment she had seen him. This had been the promise, the possibility, that had always, surely, been meant to ripen to reality.

She wanted this man, wanted him with a blind, hot intensity that was so utterly different from her feeling for Anthony that it would never have occurred to her to call it by the same name. And he wanted her too. She knew it with every atom of her body, and every part of her seemed to leap and rejoice at the knowledge that he meant them to belong to each other.

Then, as suddenly, he was releasing her, not angrily, but with an infinite gentleness. She could see his face change, slowly and inexorably, as his self-control came back to him.

'God help Downing if you do marry him,' he said harshly. 'He'll never be the man for you, not in a thousand years. Now get on the phone, and come and tell me when you've got me a room. You'll find me back in the Rose Room.'

He didn't slam the door; he opened it softly, with the same iron-clad control, and closed it in just the same manner, leaving Laura alone in the study.

Finding Alex a hotel room was more of a chore than he had perhaps realised. In the middle of summer all the good local hotels were booked solid with holiday-makers months in advance, and Laura guessed that he wouldn't appreciate the kind of English pub where the bathroom was along the corridor and the water generally freezing. She had to phone all the decent hotels in Cirencester, then all those in Stroud, before she finally found a double room in a country hotel nearly ten miles from Exonby. The price was astronomical, but she told herself that Alex would have no trouble in affording it, and booked it—not knowing what his plans were—provisionally for two weeks.

When she returned to the Rose Room to give him the details, the large, elegant room had almost emptied. The hired waitresses were bustling around collecting empty sherry glasses. Lady Exonby, looking frail and tired, was sitting with Lady Downing in a pair of chairs near the window. Alex and Anthony were standing side by side in front of the fireplace, very obviously not talking to each other, and Lord and Lady Mallingham, her own parents, were a few feet away, watching the door anxiously as if they had been waiting for her to return.

Lady Exonby beckoned her over immediately, and she felt obliged to ignore the looks from the others—not that Alex looked her way at all—and hurry over to see what her employer needed.

'Laura, my dear,' Lady Exonby said as soon as she was within earshot, 'perhaps you can make my nephew see sense where I've failed. Please explain to him that it will not upset me in the slightest if he takes the Blue Room. He seems to imagine that I'm mourning the loss of my house, but, as I've known for the last seventy years that I'd have to move out as soon as George died, that really is ridiculous of him.'

Laura's heart sank. 'You're absolutely right, Lady Exonby,' she said reassuringly, 'but I've already spoken to his lordship, and it seems they do things differently in New Mexico.'

'My dear girl, we are not in New Mexico. We are in Gloucestershire.'

'And if you'll forgive my saying so, Lady Exonby, you must be quite exhausted after the strain of the funeral. Won't you let me see you to your room? Or shall I call Mrs Mason and ask her to see to you?'

Lady Exonby shook her head. 'Mason and Mrs Mason are both seeing to the overnight guests, and I shall stay here for as long as my other guests are here.'

'Florry, we really must be going,' Lady Downing put in.

'Then let me see you out.' Lady Exonby stood up, with deliberate dignity, and offered her hand to the other woman.

Laura glanced at Anthony, who grimaced back at her. She knew he had wanted a word with her after the funeral, but it wasn't possible for her to speak to him with Alex there, and fortunately he seemed to realise that. Her father moved across, murmured that they must be going too, and promised to call her later that evening.

Only moments later, the Downings and the Mallinghams were all saying goodbye to Lady Exonby in the hallway, and Laura found herself alone again with Alex.

'So where am I staying?' he asked curtly.

She thought of making a last attempt to persuade him to stay at the Hall, but she felt sure that she hadn't a hope of succeeding. 'It's called The Chequers,' she said. 'It's a ten-mile drive, so I'd better find a map and show you the way.'

'Just give me the address, and I'll find it.'

She had it written down, and she handed the paper over to him just as Lady Exonby came back into the room.

'Now, young man,' Lady Exonby said imperiously, 'dinner is served at seven. I'll ring for Mason, and he can show you to your room.'

'That's thoughtful of you, ma'am, but I'll eat at my hotel. Laura, I'll phone you tomorrow.' Alex reached out, just touched Laura's hand, and strode out of the room before either woman could say another word.

CHAPTER SEVEN

THREE days later—on Monday morning—Laura sat apprehensively in the study at Exonby Hall, waiting for the new earl to arrive.

She had not seen Alex since the funeral breakfast. The following morning he had telephoned her. He'd asked her to come over to The Chequers and have lunch with him, and she had refused. She had been needed at the Hall that day, and had promised to spend Sunday at Maltwood House with Anthony. Anyway, he should have come over to the Hall, as Lady Exonby wanted him to do. She had told him this, and he'd put the receiver down.

Half an hour later he'd phoned her again—brusquely formal this time, with instructions for her. On Monday he would come to the Hall. He wanted to look over this and this information, to interview this and this person. Would she arrange it all for him, please? Thank you and goodbye.

She'd phoned him back, three times, not least to try and pass on Lady Exonby's invitation to dinner. But each time the hotel receptionist had told her sweetly that Mr Gillon—he had evidently not registered under his new title—had said he was not accepting incoming calls.

Curse him! He was behaving abominably. It was a tiny consolation that he was at least coming to the Hall, was showing some interest in the estate affairs. But it wasn't enough, as Lady Exonby had complained to her at great length all weekend.

116

It hadn't been easy to do as he had asked, either. He wanted so much information. He expected so many people to be at hand, at such short notice. He seemed to expect to gallop through all the formalities of inheriting the estate, but he would have to learn that in England the legal system couldn't be hurried.

It would take several weeks, she reckoned, for him to find his way around the estate and its business affairs, to meet all the staff and the professional advisers. Perhaps in those long weeks of later summer, his antagonism to Exonby would fade. Perhaps he would decide to stay, after all. Perhaps he and she would——

Stop it, Laura, she told herself. She was Anthony's fiancée. They might be going through a bad patch, but they were still firmly committed to each other. Anthony was a fine man, and as for Alex—she wasn't yet sure that she knew what he was in the slightest.

Ten to nine. She shuffled her sheaf of papers nervously, and went to check the filter coffee machine for the fourth time. Even if Alex didn't need plenty of cups of strong coffee to see him through the day, she was very sure she would need them herself!

At two minutes to nine, she heard the crunch of a car on the gravel outside. She went to the window, peered out, and saw the Ford that had been parked outside the main entrance after the funeral pulling up once more in precisely the same place. As she watched, Alex climbed out, slammed the car door behind him, and strode up the steps towards the doors. He was wearing a grey business suit, his gold-brown hair ruffled by the light breeze, his vigour and impatience undimmed by the glass through which she was watching him.

She didn't go to let him in. That was Mason's job. He would have to wait while Mason made his way to the hall. He would have to reply—politely, she hoped—to all Mason's small talk. It would do him good; he needed to relearn how things were done at Exonby.

Deliberately, she fed a clean sheet of paper into her typewriter, switched it on, and began to type out the start of a letter.

Tap, tap, tap. That was Mason's usual discreet knock. She turned the typewriter off unhurriedly, and called out, 'Yes, Mason?'

'His lordship is here, Lady Laura.'

'Show him in, Mason.'

'This way, your lordship.'

'Mason, my name is Alex, or Mr Gillon if you prefer, and I will not, not, repeat not, be called your lordship by you or by anyone else. Do you understand?'

Laura heard Mason's subdued voice muttering, 'As you wish, sir,' and had to suppress a smile. Alex Gillon certainly wasn't a man who made life easy for himself, or for those around him. He could go on reminding Mason till the butler was ninety, and she was willing to bet that Mason would *still* be calling him 'your lordship'!

She stood up, keeping her back firmly against the typing table for protection. The door to the study opened, and Alex strode in.

'Good morning, your lordship.'

He stopped still, and for a moment she thought he was going to bawl her out. Then he strode past her towards the main desk with deliberate casualness, turned, and said in a cool voice, 'The first thing you can do for me this morning is to find out how on earth I can get rid of this damn title.'

'It's generally thought to be a privilege to possess an earldom.'

'Not by anybody with sense. Is there any coffee going round here?'

'It's freshly brewed. How do you take it?'

'Black, no sugar.'

She went to pour it. Behind her, she could hear the scrape of a chair being pulled out from under the big desk, and the rustle of papers.

When she turned round, with a coffee-cup in either hand, Alex was standing by the desk and frowning down at the schedule of appointments that she had typed out for him the previous day.

'Thanks,' he said absently, as she put his cup down on the desk-top. 'I thought I said I wanted to see Exonby's solicitor first thing.'

'You did, but Mr Flowerdew is in court all day today. If you look at the next sheet, you'll see that I've made an appointment for him to come here on Thursday.'

'Thursday! But that's three days off!'

'So it is,' Laura agreed.

'Get him on the phone now.'

'I can try if you insist, but most likely he's halfway down the Gloucester Road by now. Shall I call his secretary?'

'Oh, leave it.' He looked up at her, and held her eyes for a moment, intently. For an instant she expected him to smile, but his severe expression didn't waver. He returned to the paper. 'You've fixed nothing before midday?'

'I thought you'd maybe prefer to go through the estate papers with me this morning. That'll give you an overview of the situation, before you interview the land agents and the chief tenants this afternoon.'

'Makes sense.' Alex dragged round the desk chair, and sat down on it, heavily. 'Let's get started, then.'

For the next three hours they worked together, intently, pausing only to refill their coffee-cups at regular intervals. It wasn't much like working with Lady Exonby. Where Lady Exonby would often take half an hour or more considering the perfect wording to a letter, Alex stormed on ahead, making rapid decisions, dictating letters at a pace that had Laura stretched to her limits, and asking question after question.

He wanted to know everything: rents, salaries, income from shooting rights and fishing rights and guided tours around the house on open days, patterns of investments and their yields. Laura answered him as best she could. She had expected to be able to answer his every question, but she found she couldn't; he looked at things from angles that she simply hadn't anticipated.

He might claim to be useless with figures, but that didn't mean he couldn't read a balance sheet. He steadily tore apart the last two years' accounts for the estate, explaining occasionally what he was doing via a few terse asides.

Maybe it was true, Laura thought, that Exonby as a place didn't interest him. But business, all business, did interest him, and he didn't feign boredom with the morning's work. He seemed particularly absorbed in tracking down the activities that were losing money. She already knew about some of them. Some of the tenanted farms had needed heavy repairs which exceeded their rent bills. A huge assortment of local organisations had used the parkland, from the pony club with their annual gymkhana to the Guides camping in the woodland, and Lord and Lady Exonby had made no attempt to charge them a commercial rate.

Others were less expected. Alex lingered over the income from the tours of the Hall. 'All right,' Laura said exasperatedly, 'we all know that it doesn't cover the running costs of the entire household. But it's a public service, Alex, and it does make a useful contribution.'

'Does it? *Does* it?'

'Well, of course it does. You can see it here: the income from the tours was more than three times the cost of the guides.'

'Yes, but the guides' salaries aren't the only overhead created by the tours. Guides, OK.' He wrote down a figure on a clean sheet of paper. 'But how about additional cleaning costs?'

'That's not easy to quantify.'

'Let's say, a tenth of the overall cleaners' bill. That's on the low side, wouldn't you agree?' He leafed through the ledgers, and added another figure. 'Insurance costs?'

'Oh, for heaven's sake!'

'For heaven's sake what? Doesn't it cost more to insure a house that's open to the public? Then what about wear and tear, breakages, advertising costs? Where are all those?'

Inexorably, he added to the list. He was fair, rational, and Laura had to admit that he was right; he proved beyond question that to open the house was not earning the estate money, but costing it several thousand pounds each year.

They did more than Laura would have believed possible by lunchtime, but it was clear that there was still far more to be done. 'We'll get back to this tomorrow,' Alex said, shutting the final ledger with a bang. 'What are the plans for lunch?'

'You've a working lunch with representatives of the land agents, and a group of the farm tenants. Here's the guest list. Then after lunch they each have an individual appointment to see you.'

Alex's eyes rapidly scanned the list. They came to a dead halt near the bottom, as Laura had anticipated.

'What's this supposed to mean?'

'What's what supposed to mean?' she asked innocently.

'This entry here. 4 p.m., Lady Exonby.'

'Oh. Lady Exonby asked me to make an appointment for her with you. At teatime, she thought, but she won't force you to drink any if you'd rather not.'

'An appointment!'

'Well, Alex, you've been in England four days and not given her a single chance to talk to you. And she's not having that.'

Alex stared at her. Laura looked calmly back. She knew Lady Exonby would insist on his keeping the appointment. Whatever his motives, Alex was at Exonby now, and between them they would somehow corral him into playing his proper role.

He threw the list down on to the desk without further comment. 'Lunch is in the Oak Dining-Room?'

'That's right.'

'Let's go, then.'

'I'll show you the way,' Laura said, getting to her feet and flexing leg muscles cramped by the long morning's work, 'but I won't be joining you. I'll have lunch with Lady Exonby up in her room.'

'Does she need you for anything in particular?'

'No, but normally I——'

'Well, I do need you. So you'll join us, please.'

Laura simply stared at him. Alex seemed to take in her message, because he frowned, and then said in a gentler voice, 'Laura, we haven't yet discussed your terms of employment, but I'll need a full-time secretary while I'm over here, and I was assuming that you'd act as one for me. If you'd rather not, then you'd better say so now. I guess I could hire another girl with no trouble.'

'Another girl wouldn't know her way around the estate papers.'

'That's true. So you'll work for me? I haven't gone into the question of the estate workers yet, but obviously I'll employ them all, at least for the time being. And I'll ensure you're properly paid for whatever you do.'

'I'm paid perfectly adequately at the moment,' Laura said stiffly.

'I sure hope so.' Alex picked up his suit jacket, which he had relegated to the back of his chair hours before, slung it over his shoulder, and set off towards the Oak Dining-Room.

Laura followed him—at a distance—down the corridor. She glowered at his back. So much for her fears that he would overwhelm her with passionate overtures! There hadn't been a pleasant, let alone a loving, word or gesture from him all morning.

In fact, working for him was going to be sheer hell, if the morning had been a fair sample. Why on earth had she agreed to continue?

Because it's in Exonby's interests, she told herself sternly. He still has to be persuaded to keep the estate running in much the same way as before. I'm in a better position than anybody else to persuade him.

But there was another reason. Though the morning had been tough, it had fired her enthusiasm in a way that the slow days working with Lady Exonby had never done. Her mind still seemed to be functioning at double speed, and there was a spring in her step as she tracked Alex's lanky figure until he paused, temporarily stumped, in the hallway, waiting for her to catch up and remind him of the way to the dining-room.

Alex's working lunch was conducted in the same vigorous manner as his rifle through the ledgers. He refused the wine that Mason offered—and most of the tenants sheepishly followed suit—did speedy justice to the ham salad, then set down to business. Laura sat at his left—after a rapid dash upstairs to explain her absence to Lady Exonby—and made notes for him.

She had met all the men at the table before, but it seemed to her now that she'd never seen them so clearly before. Never before had she thought to judge their competence. Now she seemed to see them through Alex's eyes, and she found it surprisingly easy to work out which men he would favour, and which he would cold-shoulder, where he would take information on trust, and where he would double-check it for himself.

He began the meal by telling the men that he preferred to be called 'Gillon', but to her relief he didn't insist on the point as he had done with her and with Mason, or correct them when some of them called him 'your lordship'. His manner was cool and formal, and most of them picked up his tone and echoed it.

He dominated the gathering, but in spite of his casual clothes—only he was in shirt sleeves; all the other men were formally dressed—and his air of authority, he wasn't relaxed; he was brusque, almost edgy throughout.

To the others, Laura suspected, this edginess would come across as sheer energy, but she herself read something different into it: nervous tension. Alex had been tense even in New Mexico, but he was far less at home here than he had been in New Mexico. He wouldn't laugh here; he wouldn't know how to tell jokes here. He seemed to be perpetually on guard. She couldn't help remembering the cleaner's comments about Maud Higgins' boy, and wondering, not for the first time, whether something similar had prompted his original decision to emigrate.

From what Anthony had said, she couldn't see him as a victim of school bullies; she suspected he had always held a firm upper hand. But perhaps he had never really identified with schoolmates such as Anthony, who came from more conventional upper-class backgrounds? Perhaps he had always felt ill at ease on those childhood visits to Exonby?

What she and Lady Exonby needed to do, Laura thought, was to make him feel at home. They needed to help him relax here, to feel a part of Gloucestershire society. If they managed to do that, then surely he would accept his obligation to remain at Exonby. But how? She might have identified the problem, but she knew that wasn't remotely the same as solving it.

The afternoon passed in a rush, with Laura perpetually seeing one interviewee into the study and another one out. The atmosphere in the Rose Room grew thick with cigarette smoke, as the men who were waiting to see Alex paced up and down like students about to sit a difficult exam. Her head began to ache.

It was a relief when four o'clock came, and she could see the last tenant to the door. Alex had interviewed them all precisely on schedule.

'That's it,' she said briskly, returning to the study where Alex, who was showing not the remotest sign of weariness, was frowning as he jotted down figures on a large pad of paper. 'Are you ready for me to show you up to Lady Exonby, or would you like a few minutes' break first?'

'I'll come now.'

They walked in silence down the familiar corridors and up the familiar staircases. Laura didn't know what to say, and Alex didn't seem to have anything to say. They reached the door of Lady Exonby's private sitting-room, and Laura knocked.

'Mr Gillon is here, your ladyship.'

When she opened the door, Lady Exonby raised one-arched eyebrow, as if she disapproved of Laura calling him by that name. 'Thank you, Laura.'

Laura stepped into the room, and Alex followed her.

'I'll make sure his lordship is shown back down to the study when we've finished,' Lady Exonby said.

Wasn't she to stay? Laura stared at Lady Exonby, then turned and glanced at Alex. He said nothing. Quietly, she edged out of the room.

There was no reason for her to stay, she told herself firmly, as she retraced her steps. Lady Exonby obviously wanted to talk to her nephew in private. Maybe she had confided heavily in Laura over the previous few weeks, but that didn't make Laura one of the family. But all the same, she minded being excluded. She minded not knowing what Alex and his aunt were saying to each other.

Angrily, she poured herself another cup of strong coffee, knocked it back in two gulps, then sat down at her typewriter and began to transcribe some of the endless pages of scribbled notes she had made since nine o'clock that morning.

Over the next week, Alex and Laura fell into a steady pattern of work. Alex went through the estate accounts, line by line. He interviewed every employee and tenant of the estate. He talked to Jeremy Flowerdew, the Exonbys' solicitor, to the accountant who handled the estate affairs, and to an endless assortment of men from the tax office and the VAT office and various Government departments which had allocated grants to the estate.

He dictated endless notes and letters to Laura, and whenever she had a spare moment she sat down to type them up.

He also doubled her pay, and, feeling that she deserved every penny, she didn't quibble with his judgement.

Everything he did was logical and sensible; everything was done with the incisive common sense that had made him a fortune back in New Mexico. On a practical level, he and Laura seemed to communicate admirably. But all the time she was conscious that his mental barriers were up high against her. She somehow couldn't bring herself to ask him what he made of Exonby now, or how his future plans were taking shape.

Except for a couple of times when he lost his temper, he made an effort to be a thoughtful and courteous, as well as a demanding, boss. But he didn't make any effort at all to be anything more to her. He never even held her eyes or smiled, let alone touched or kissed her. He didn't speak again of his reasons for coming to Exonby, or of his feelings for her.

Perhaps he really didn't have any? Laura asked herself this sometimes, but she didn't believe it. What she did believe was that Alex was inhibited from making any more advances to her, because she was—still—Anthony's fiancée.

Had Alex really thought she would break her engagement as soon as he followed her to England? She had no idea. But she hadn't done it, and she hadn't any intention of doing it.

Any intention? Perhaps that wasn't entirely true. She didn't deny to herself that Alex attracted her more and more strongly, though she tried to school herself not to let her eyes rest on his tall figure too often. She couldn't help thinking sometimes that, if he were to stay on at Exonby, she would find it intolerably difficult to cope with being his neighbour, Lady Downing, and nothing more to him. But he hadn't given her any indication that that was what he intended. And unless it was what he intended, there obviously couldn't be any future for the two of them.

Really, she wanted to wait and see how things developed. Sometimes she thought this was an admirably sensible approach, and sometimes she worried that it was prompted by weak and unworthy motives. Did she really want to marry Anthony, sufficient to justify going ahead? She wasn't sure. But then, did she not want to marry Anthony, sufficient to justify breaking the commitment she had already made to him? She wasn't sure about that, either.

It was particularly hard to decide either way, when she really wasn't seeing anything of Anthony. With Alex blasting his way through Exonby's records and accounts, demanding her help and assistance at every step, she hadn't time to go over to Maltwood for the occasional lazy evening with Anthony. Lady Downing had started—to her embarrassment—to prepare for their planned autumn wedding, getting quotes from caterers and florists and hirers of marquees, but she really didn't have time to participate in this activity either.

Perhaps waiting and seeing wasn't the wisest course, if she was going to find herself swept unavoidably towards her wedding-day with Anthony before she had had a chance to consider the alternatives properly. But what else was she to do?

Early in the second week of his stay, Alex told Laura to confirm his return flight to Albuquerque for the Friday of the following week.

Laura simply stared at him for a moment. He was going back to New Mexico?

But of course he was, she told herself firmly. He was still the boss of Northways, and he had left for England at very short notice. Whatever his future plans, it made sense for him to return to New Mexico at that time. His face wasn't inviting questions, and she didn't ask any. She simply phoned the travel agency and did as he had asked. As soon as he had left the Hall that afternoon— he had insisted on continuing to stay at The Chequers— she went to tell Lady Exonby of his plans.

'So when is he planning to come back again?' Lady Exonby asked thoughtfully.

'He hasn't mentioned it. I doubt if he'll want to come back until all the legal formalities have been completed. The rest of this week and next will give him time to do all that he's free to do before Exonby is formally his.'

'That's true,' his aunt agreed. They were both silent for a moment, both thinking—Laura assumed—how different things might be when Lady Exonby was settled in the Dower House, and Alex ran the estate. Then Lady Exonby said brusquely, 'If he hasn't yet fixed a date, then we'll have to hold a proper dinner before he goes. For the neighbours.'

'Do you think he'd agree to hold one?' Laura asked dubiously.

'My dear,' Lady Exonby retorted, 'I am not totally unable to handle my nephew.'

The next day Alex was summoned upstairs to her sitting-room. He came back to the study half an hour later, stony-faced, and threw a piece of paper on to Laura's desk.

'You'd better invite these people to dinner next Wednesday.'

'Should I write to them, or phone them?'

'Do whatever you normally do.'

She barely heard him, since she was busily reading the list. It was in Lady Exonby's handwriting, and there were twenty names on it. Lady Exonby's wasn't one of them. Of course, the dinner would be less than a month after her husband's funeral, so she could be forgiven for opting out of it.

There was Alex's name, and Laura's own, Sir Anthony and Lady Downing, the vicar of Exonby Church and his wife, and a selection of local landowners and their wives. Apart from Alex himself, everybody on the list was a regular visitor to the Hall.

Even so, it wasn't what she had expected. She looked up at Alex. He was standing by the desk that had once been Lady Exonby's, and had now effectively become his, and was staring out of the window. His brows were lowered, and for once he looked, not vigorous and determined, but thoroughly weary. Seeing him in profile, with shoulders slightly slumped and mouth set in a thin line, she was reminded, for the first time in days, of his dead uncle.

Should she say something? He would probably be angry with her if she did. He was tired, too tired to take her suggestion calmly. And Lady Exonby would probably be none too pleased if he acted on it.

But this won't be Lady Exonby's dinner, she thought. It's supposed to be Alex's dinner, the first time he has entertained his neighbours as the head of the Gillon family. Lady Exonby might have a blind spot over the Gillon family, but I don't, and I can see what is proper and necessary.

'Alex?' she said tentatively.

He swung round, rapidly, to confront her. 'Yes?'

'It's not really my place to suggest this, I know, but...'

'Yes?'

'I think you ought to invite your mother and her husband to this dinner.'

She had expected him to be surprised, expected him to be annoyed. But she hadn't expected him to be completely and utterly thrown by her suggestion.

She had never seen him at a total loss before, never before seen him lose his self-control so completely. For an instant, the man confronting her wasn't the arrogant, self-possessed head of a massive business enterprise, the man so confident of himself that he could afford to scoff at an English earldom. This Alex was raw, vulnerable and sensitive. Too late, she realised that her suggestion had hurt him badly.

He recovered rapidly. 'No,' he said curtly.

For an instant, Laura was tempted to drop the suggestion. But it seemed to her that it was important. 'Look,' she went on, 'I know you're not close to your mother——'

'Not close! Good God, I haven't seen her in twenty years!'

'But she did come to the funeral. Maybe you didn't realise that. She came, and Mr Eyre, her husband, and Fenella too. They didn't come back here for the funeral breakfast, so you won't have seen them. Everybody else met them then, though, all the people who'll be coming on Wednesday, and I think it would be only proper if you invited them to come. Maybe not Fenella, but Mr and Mrs Eyre, at least.'

'I said no.' Alex turned away from her, and picked up a couple of papers from his desk.

'You won't have to see them again for another twenty years if you don't want to,' Laura went on. 'But don't you see? Just this once, you really do have to invite them.'

'Drop it, Laura,' Alex said in a tight voice.

Laura opened her mouth to argue. But then she saw the suppressed anger on Alex's face, and she knew that she didn't dare to press him any further.

'If you say so,' she said quietly. 'I'll leave you to work here, and go and make these phone calls from the Rose Room.'

'Tell you what,' Anthony said on the phone the following day, 'come over here, say at five-ish, on Wednesday afternoon. You can change here, have a couple of sherries with Mother and me and we'll all drive over to Exonby for this dinner afterwards.'

'But Anthony,' Laura protested, 'I won't possibly have time to do that!'

'You've got to make *some* time, Laura. Mother has all sorts of arrangements to go through with you. Anyway, even if you are living at Exonby at the moment, you're my fiancée, and I want you to come to this dinner with me, properly, like the guest you are.'

'But I'm not exactly a guest at it, Anthony.'

'Then you jolly well should be!'

'You may think so, but you have to understand, Anthony, that Alex is a single man who doesn't know anybody in Gloucestershire. He needs somebody to act as his hostess for this dinner, and there really isn't anybody else who can do it.'

There was silence at the other end of the telephone. Then, 'Laura,' Anthony said, in a cold voice, 'you are *my* fiancée and I insist that you come to this dinner as my fiancée. I don't care how much work you're doing for Lord Exonby on the estate affairs at the moment, I am not going to escort my mother to dinner at Exonby Hall while you act as hostess for another man.'

'I'm sorry, Anthony, but you'll just have to accept it.'

Anthony began on another ponderous protest, but Laura, feeling acutely guilty, had already put down the phone on him.

CHAPTER EIGHT

LAURA'S dress was of yellow taffeta, with a very full skirt and a low-cut square bodice. Mrs Mason, the housekeeper, had helped her put up her hair, and now she was putting the finishing touches to her make-up. She slipped on to her wrist a heavy gold bracelet, set with pearls to match her choker, and stood up to check her reflection in the mirror. Her skirt swirled as she moved, and caught the light in dramatic glints and folds. She looked bright-eyed and flushed with excitement.

It would have been impossible not to be excited at the thought of the dinner, when the whole of Exonby Hall had been in a frenzy all day. The best silver had been taken out of the bank vaults, and polished by the kitchen staff. Lady Exonby had spent hours discussing the menu with Mrs Mason and the caterers. Mason had spent almost as many hours in the cellars, dusting down bottles of the very best claret and, at Lady Exonby's suggestion, of champagne for cocktails. It would be the grandest dinner that had been held at the Hall for years, and certainly by far the grandest since Laura had come to work there.

And she was to act as hostess, in the teeth of Anthony's furious objections. It would be her job to greet the guests, and introduce those of them he did not already know to Alex. It would be her job to keep the conversation flowing smoothly, to ensure that the staff performed to perfection, and to somehow make sure that the ill feeling between Alex and Anthony was kept well beneath the surface all evening.

The last of these would be the real problem, because she was painfully aware that Anthony at least had some reason to be annoyed. It was true that she hadn't paid him the attention he could reasonably have expected since Alex's arrival. It was true that Alex still attracted her intensely. Anthony wasn't a particularly intuitive man, but he would be looking for signs of that attraction, and she wasn't at all certain that she would be able to hide it successfully.

But all Anthony's wilder fears were a very long way from being realised. He probably imagined all kinds of passionate interludes between her and Alex, while in fact there hadn't been a word or touch he could have objected to since the day of the old earl's funeral.

If Anthony might find that hard to believe, she found it almost as hard to believe herself. At first Alex had seemed to make it so clear that he wanted her. Their attraction to each other had been irresistible. But if Alex still felt that attraction, he had been resisting it very effectively for the previous fortnight.

Was that because she was still engaged to Anthony? As the days had gone by, she had become increasingly unsure. Alex didn't seem to her the kind of man who would stand by while the woman he wanted for himself prepared to marry another man. At first he had given every indication that he was prepared to fight Anthony for her. But he hadn't fought. He hadn't offered her himself and Exonby, as alternative to Anthony and Maltwood. He hadn't given her the remotest clue what his real intentions were.

Was he really leaving it to her? Was he expecting her to take a leap in the dark and end her engagement to Anthony without any encouragement from him? Perhaps he was.

And perhaps she would do it. Deep down inside, she knew that she wanted to be Alex's wife, the Countess of Exonby, with a hot hunger that the prospect of becoming Anthony's wife had never stirred in her. Marriage to Anthony would be pleasant but dull; marriage to Alex would give her a thousand times more. If she hesitated to take that leap, wasn't it basically from cowardice, from nothing more worthy than the fear that she would be made to look a fool if she proved to have judged him wrong? Or was it from more admirable motives, like reluctance to cause Anthony and his family unjustified hurt?

Only one thing she knew for sure. It was Wednesday evening, and Alex was leaving early on Friday. Time was running out for them both. Her first duty was to ensure that the dinner party was a triumph for Exonby; but her second, and even harder task, was to make that difficult decision whether to break with Anthony. She prayed that Alex would give her the guidance she so badly needed.

She shook her head, making her long drop earrings quiver, and made for her bedroom door.

Alex was standing in the hallway when she reached the landing. She leaned over the banisters and saw him there, looking handsome and assured in his evening dress, talking to Mason. Her breath caught, and she stayed there for a moment, guiltily enjoying the pleasure of staring at him without his knowing it.

The glint of her dress must have caught the edge of his attention, though, because a moment later he looked up and saw her. He stood still, watching her, as she made her way nervously down the stairs to join him.

'You're looking very lovely, Laura,' he said in a low voice.

It was a trite compliment, but all the same it was the first that he had paid her since he had come to Exonby. She felt herself colouring. It pleased her so much, and yet she didn't dare to read too much into it.

'Everything's ready,' he went on. 'Shall we go into the Rose Room?'

He held out his arm, and she took it. They walked together through the wide doorway to the Rose Room. Drinks and glasses had been set out on a long sideboard, and a waitress was bustling around making her final preparations.

'What'll you drink? Shall we open some champagne now?'

She shook her head. 'Just water for now, thank you.'

'No way. One glass of champagne right now won't hurt you. May I?' He said this to the waitress, as he reached past her to the nearest of the champagne bottles. He ripped off the foil, levered the cork out with easy competence, and Laura rushed to grab a couple of glasses and catch the overflow as the contents fizzed out of the bottle.

'Thank you,' Alex said. He put the bottle down, and took a glass from her. Their hands just touched. He raised his glass, and Laura followed suit with hers.

'We need a toast,' Laura said. 'To the Fourth Earl of Exonby? No, you won't drink to that, will you? To Exonby Hall?'

'To you and me,' Alex responded, in a firm voice.

This time she couldn't avoid his eyes. They held her, enfolded her, trapped her. The world seemed to have narrowed to the two of them, caught in a place beyond time. He wasn't touching her in any way, but that made no difference to the intense intimacy of the moment.

It was Alex who broke it, by clinking his glass against hers, and drinking down the champagne. 'To us,' Laura faintly echoed, and she followed suit.

'Your lordship,' Mason politely interrupted, 'the Reverend and Mrs Smith have arrived.'

*   *   *

The setting for the dinner, in the Oak Dining-Room, with candles blazing from the tall silver candlesticks and the flames reflected on the silver, the cut glass, and more faintly in the polished oak panels lining the walls, could not have been more perfect. The food was excellent, the wine superb, the guests were charming and civilised.

But to Laura, the evening was an ordeal almost from the start.

She had made her decision. She had made it the very moment Alex had proposed his toast. Perhaps the toast hadn't meant absolutely all that she had hoped it meant, but whether Alex asked her to marry him or not she knew that it would be wrong for her to marry Anthony. She didn't love him, not in the way that a wife ought to love a husband, and now she knew it. Now she knew what she had not known when she had accepted his proposal: what it was like to ache for a man's embrace.

She knew that she hadn't any option but to keep her decision to herself until she had a suitable opportunity to end her engagement with Anthony, and it was a strain, of course, accepting his attentions while she was longing to put her choice into effect, and to ally herself openly with Alex. But there was another problem, too.

There was Alex himself.

Alex looked his best in his classic evening dress. It was precisely what he had been wearing when she had first met him, and it was inevitable that this formal occasion should bring with it reminders of the ball at the Marbury Motel. She hadn't been prepared, though, for the real contrast between the two occasions.

At the Marbury, Alex had been in his element. He had been among friends, in a community where he was accepted as a leading figure. It had been obvious even to an outsider like her how widely he was admired and respected, and his after-dinner speech had been a *tour de force*.

At Exonby, Alex was like a fish out of water.

Oh, he was still a handsome, intelligent, forceful man. His manners were impeccable. He didn't use the wrong knives and forks, or get disgracefully drunk, or otherwise make a fool of himself. He was the Earl of Exonby, their host for the evening, and his neighbours treated him with polite deference as their social superior. But he didn't seem to be able to accept their deferential attentions in the correct light, self-deprecating manner, and he didn't seem to be able to judge how to treat them in return.

The trouble was, Laura thought wretchedly, watching him stumble through a conversation with the Lord Lieutenant's wife, that his guests had arrived expecting to meet the Earl of Exonby, and that Alex was acting— as always—like Alex Gillon, successful garage owner from New Mexico. He couldn't, or wouldn't, play this other role.

His guests were all part of the tightly knit social circle of landed Gloucestershire. Laura couldn't help remembering the vicious remarks he had made to her about English society, back in New Mexico. These people were precisely the type of people he had described then. They all had easy lifestyles and moderate ambitions. They weren't go-getters, they didn't aim to make a huge fortune or leave any indelible mark on the world. They were pleasant, considerate, well-intentioned people. They were the sort of people she had lived with all her life, people she knew and liked and respected. Alex didn't know them. He didn't seem to like them. And, though he was superficially polite to them, she sensed that he didn't feel the slightest respect for them and their achievements.

They did respect him, but not, Laura came increasingly to realise as the evening wore on, for the achievements he was used to being respected for. What they looked up to was his position as head of an aristocratic

English family. They knew he ran a substantial business in New Mexico, but they really weren't interested in Northways Garages. Many of them, she realised, secretly thought of running a chain of garages as a rather dirty, vulgar occupation, not really fitting for an earl. Their attitude suggested that there was something shameful about making millions and employing hundreds of people.

These struck her as very real problems. If she was right—and she hoped with all her heart that she was—then Alex would be marrying her, and living at Exonby in future. He would be mixing with these people for the rest of his life. Things would ease, doubtless, when he got to know them better, and they him, but she knew that it would be a long and difficult task to bridge the gap between their attitudes and his.

She prided herself on being realistic, and she had never thought of marriage—even to an earl—as a fairy-tale existence without any tensions and difficulties, but it was disturbing to realise just how large a task she would be taking on. And there was yet another problem.

Anthony had brought it to the fore. While Alex kept whatever jealousy he might feel of Laura's fiancé well hidden, Anthony seemed unable to follow suit, and all evening he indulged in sly little digs at Alex's expense. He picked on Alex's mother's family as an obvious chink in his rival's armour, and he lost no opportunity to mention them. Had Alex seen his mother and her family? Where was it they lived? What was it his stepfather did for a living? Did Alex get on well with them? And on and on.

There really wasn't anything for Alex to be ashamed of, Laura thought furiously. Maud's family might not be aristocratic, but even Anthony wasn't able to suggest that they were particularly disreputable. She reckoned things would have been much easier if Alex had followed her advice and invited the Eyres, but it was far from being a scandal that he hadn't. The trouble was that Anthony's digs really did seem to affect Alex. He managed to reply levelly to even the most pointed and stupid questions, but she sensed him growing more and more tense as the dinner progressed.

It was an unqualified relief when she found herself saying goodnight to Lord and Lady Fanshawe. Apart from Anthony and his mother, they were the last remaining guests, and she made her way back to the Rose Room, where they had returned after the meal, knowing that in a few minutes the ordeal would be over.

But there was still a particularly awkward part of it to face. The atmosphere in the Rose Room was cold enough to freeze a furnace. Alex was propping up the mantelpiece, with a rigidly blank expression on his face. Anthony was still lingering over his third port, and Lady Downing was sitting anxiously on the edge of her chair.

Laura smiled as brightly as she could manage at Lady Downing, then turned her attention to Anthony. She felt a little wave of venomous hatred pass through her.

Of what? Maybe she had never felt passionate about her fiancé, but she had never, ever hated him! Her feelings had always been as warm as they were moderate.

But her distaste was well justified, as a moment's thought showed clearly to her. There hadn't been the slightest thing to admire in Anthony's conduct that evening. His jealousy might be forgivable, but not the petty spitefulness with which he had done his utmost to do his rival down.

The chair next to Anthony was empty, but she couldn't bring herself to take it, and she sat down instead next to Lady Downing.

'Well,' Anthony said, 'we ought to be making tracks shortly.'

'It's been a delightful evening, Alex,' Lady Downing said politely. She managed a thin smile at her stony-faced host.

It'll be over soon, Laura reminded herself. We've stuck it out so far; we mustn't give up now. She forced out a smile too, and said brightly, 'I must remember to congratulate the Masons in the morning.'

'I ought to do that, surely,' Alex responded.

'We can both do it.' She tried to catch his eye and convey her support, but he wouldn't look at her, and she was conscious of Anthony stiffening as she spoke of herself and Alex as 'we'. She felt sure he would say or do something to assert his own claim on her, so it was no surprise when he intervened, saying,

'Laura will be quite an expert at entertaining by the time we've got through our wedding reception, won't you, darling?'

'She's an excellent hostess already,' Alex retorted in a harsh voice.

Suddenly Laura could bear the artificial game no longer. She couldn't sit there, playing at being Anthony's loving fiancée and fighting to hold the smile on her aching face. She had to break the party up, even if it would be verging on rudeness.

'Actually,' she said, 'I'm a very tired hostess at the moment. I'll just have one more coffee, if there's some left, and then I'm afraid I won't be able to stay awake any longer. Lady Downing, can I get you a coffee too?'

'Oh, we should be going, my dear. It must be past one o'clock. Anthony, are you ready now?'

'I'll just say goodnight to Laura, Mother,' Anthony said. He lumbered out of his chair and crossed over to stand in front of her, in a direct line between her and Alex. He reached out a hand. Laura hesitated, but she really hadn't any alternative but to take it, and let him pull her to her feet.

She had to let Anthony lead her out of the room and into the deserted main hall. She had to let him put his arms around her. His mouth roamed wetly over her face, and found her lips with slightly drunken inaccuracy.

Anthony repelled her, made her feel physically sick. It was all she could do to hold it back, and submit woodenly to his embrace. How could I ever have welcomed his kisses? she thought, disgusted.

But then she never had welcomed them, not in the way that she had welcomed Alex's kisses. Anthony had never stirred any desire in her at all. She had thought, when she'd agreed to marry him, that that was because she wasn't a woman who could feel much desire for any man. But she had been wrong, and now she knew it. Now she knew what it was to want a man, but it was not Sir Anthony Downing whom she wanted.

The last vestiges of doubt in her mind were swept away by her disgust. She felt then that she should have ended the engagement sooner, much sooner. She had been caught in a false position ever since Alex had come to Exonby. Her hesitancy had caused nothing but pain for herself, for Alex, and for Anthony too. But at least she was resolved to put things right at the very first opportunity. She even thought of telling him her decision right then, but she knew that that would have been a shabby way of treating a man who, though he would never now be her husband, would still be her neighbour for the rest of her life.

'I wish you could come back to Maltwood with us, darling,' Anthony was whispering. 'You looked so beautiful this evening. I know it's not long till the wedding, but it seems like such an age. There really isn't any reason for us to wait until then. Come back with me tonight.'

'Anthony!' Laura struggled free from his arms, and practically pushed him away in her sudden panic. 'How could you? What—what would your mother think?'

'What would Alex Gillon think? That's what you mean, isn't it? Isn't it, Laura? I saw you tonight.' Anthony's hand grabbed at her arm, and he pulled her roughly against him. 'You could barely take your eyes off him, could you? I saw him eyeing you too. No wonder. There's bad blood there. He takes after his philandering father, not to mention that cheap slut of a mother. No better than animals, either of them, rutting with anybody who fell in their path. He's just the same. I bet he's had every housemaid in the Hall since he's been over here. But not you. I don't want him to get you, Laura. You're my woman. Mine.'

'Anthony!' Laura tried desperately to keep her voice down. She was terrified that Alex would come out of the Rose Room and see the two of them. 'Anthony, let me go this minute!'

She lashed out, with her free arm and a leg too, and for a moment they struggled silently together in the huge, empty expanse of the hall. Then Anthony released her, abruptly, and she fell a pace back, nursing her arm. It ached where he had gripped it.

'Oh, God, Laura, I'm sorry,' Anthony said sheepishly. 'I shouldn't have said those things. But it makes me insane with jealousy, knowing I've got to leave you here with him.'

'Anthony, I think you should go right now,' Laura said in an unsteady voice.

'I'd better give you a minute to recover, then I'll call Mother. Honestly, I won't touch you again. I really don't mind waiting till the wedding, Laura, you know I don't.'

There can't be a wedding, Laura thought numbly. There will never be a wedding. I'll have to drive over to Maltwood tomorrow, and tell you that then.

A moment later Anthony had reopened the door of the Rose Room, and was ushering his mother out into the hall, with Alex close behind her.

Laura kept her composure until she and Alex had seen the two of them into their car. Lady Downing was driving, and Laura waved and smiled as the car pulled away. Then she turned back to the house, and Alex, in a sudden protective gesture, put an arm across her shoulders.

The contrast between his touch, warm and reassuring, and Anthony's repulsive lunge only moments earlier was so great that she quivered. She had to fight the urge to turn to him and melt into his arms.

She couldn't. Not now. Another day, and she would have the right to love Alex without the shadow of guilt that now hung over her. Now she didn't. It wasn't long to wait. She would have to find the strength to wait somehow.

As did Alex. Once they were inside the house he moved away from her, and said curtly, 'I'll just tell Mason he can lock up now. Did you want more coffee, or are you going straight up?'

'I'll go straight up, Alex. I really am exhausted.'

'So am I.' For almost the first time that evening, he smiled—wearily, but a real smile that lit up his eyes. 'Sleep well, Laura.'

'You too.'

Laura had intended to ring Anthony first thing in the morning, but in fact she had no opportunity to do so. In her exhaustion she forgot to set her alarm clock, and she didn't wake until one of the housemaids knocked on her bedroom door at eight-thirty, with a cup of coffee and the information that his lordship had already arrived, and would be grateful if she would join him in the study as soon as possible.

Curse his lordship! she thought, her passion for Alex thoroughly subdued by her hangover. Didn't he ever feel hung over himself? Hadn't he ever heard of a lie-in, or was that another facet of the decadent English lifestyle he had left behind him?

Still, this was hardly the time to test his patience to the limits, so she gulped the coffee while dressing and pushed open the study door less than twenty minutes later.

She found Alex sitting at the desk, Biro in hand, with a frown on his face.

'Come in and sit down,' he said tersely. 'I've a lot still to do before I fly home tomorrow, so there's no time to waste.'

'Alex,' she said exasperatedly, 'it's not all that urgent. You may be going back to New Mexico tomorrow, but I'll still be here at Exonby. You don't have to dot every "i" and cross every "t" today. I'm perfectly capable of keeping things going until you get back again.'

'I shan't be coming back here again.'

There was a moment's dead silence. She was too stunned to react. And it was Alex who finally broke it, wearily getting to his feet and turning to face her. He held her eyes.

She didn't try to hide her emotions. And nor was he hiding his, for once. There was a raw current surging between them, in which desire, anger, shock and a dozen other feelings mingled inextricably.

'I told you, Laura,' he said harshly.

'Yes, but I thought ... I hoped ...'

'Then you thought wrong. And there's work to be done, so sit down, please, and we'll get started.'

Numb to the core, moving like a robot, Laura pulled out her chair and sat.

Alex's manner had already changed. Now it was as impersonal as it had been during the previous week. He sat down again, set his elbows on the desk, leaned forwards, propping his chin against his clenched fists, and said flatly, 'You already know my basic plan.'

She didn't answer, and he went on, his voice growing louder and harsher. 'I'll give Lady Exonby as long as she needs, within reason, to clear out of this place and settle into the Dower House, but I want the whole household reduced to a skeleton staff as soon as I've left. Mason and Mrs Mason should have three months' notice. That ought to mean they'll be here until you and Lady Exonby leave. You'll maybe need one housemaid too, but I want all the rest of the staff to be given a month's notice from tomorrow.'

'All of them! But, Alex!'

'Or whatever the legal requirements are. Mitchell and Harker struck me as the most efficient auctioneers, so I'll appoint them to sell off the contents. Obviously that can't be done until the will is proved, but I want it done as soon as possible afterwards.'

'*Sell* the contents?'

'Everything. Lady Exonby gets first refusal, obviously, and the other family members may want to make offers for some of the heirlooms in advance of the public auction. I'll accept any reasonable offers they make. Then I want Flowerdew to start in train right away the application for demolition of the Hall.'

'Demolition!'

'He said I might not get permission, but I want the application made immediately. If it's refused, then the agents have recommended a firm of architects who can draw up plans for its conversion into apartments. I'll give you further instructions from the States if it proves necessary.'

'Alex Gillon, you're crazy!'

'George Graham made the best proposal for the parkland. It makes sense to lease it to him, it'll add directly on to his lands at Home Farm. I'll hold back the gardens immediately round the house until I know about the demolition permission, but Flowerdew can get to work now on drawing up a lease for the rest, to run for the same term as the remainder of Graham's lease.'

'You're turning the park into farmland!'

'Only the grassland. Graham doesn't want the woods, he says lumber isn't his line. I haven't fixed on a buyer for the woodland yet. I'll have to send you instructions on how to deal with that.'

He paused for a moment. Laura, meanwhile, was fighting to keep a lid on the boiling pot of her reactions. What he was proposing was worse than her worst nightmares!

But. But he doesn't know yet, she thought. He doesn't know that I've decided to break with Anthony. This isn't really going to happen. It can't happen. Things will be entirely different once he realises that I've chosen him after all.

Why, why hadn't she woken earlier, and driven over to Maltwood first thing? Why hadn't she overcome her scruples and told Anthony the previous night? Why hadn't she put things straight between them days ago, instead of leaving it till this latest of late hours?

She hadn't. Her anger with herself was almost as great as her anger with Alex. OK, it wasn't going to happen, but that he could even *think* of it! It was appalling, horrific, unspeakable!

She wanted, more than anything, to tell him at that very moment that she had broken her engagement. But she hadn't, curse it, she hadn't! All she could do was to play for time until she had a chance to go over to Maltwood. Above all, she needed to keep him from making any irrevocable moves before she told him.

Suddenly, she saw how she might be able to do that.

'Wait a minute,' she said in a voice of dawning discovery. 'Am I supposed to take it, Alex Gillon, that you want *me* to handle all this?'

'I want you to co-ordinate it. You're the obvious person, you know most about running the place. Flowerdew and the land agents will do most of the donkey work, and you can hire anyone else you need to help you. Get permission from me first—you can fax me at Northways.'

'No.'

'Come on, Laura, you know how to work a fax machine.'

'Of course I know how to work a stupid fax machine, but there is no way I'm going to be a part of a crazy scheme like this.'

'There's nothing crazy about it,' Alex said harshly. 'It's what I've always intended to do. I told you that back in New Mexico. And even so, I've gone over every account book and every property deed in the last two weeks, and checked out every single aspect of it. It's practicable and economic and altogether the best solution.'

'The best solution! It's nothing of the kind! It's a wildly intemperate over-reaction! You haven't given yourself any time at all to come to terms with your inheritance, let alone to settle in at Exonby, and now you talk of tearing the place apart! The only "solution" is for you to cool down, and give things a chance to—well, to sort themselves out,' she ended, a little lamely.

Alex silently shook his head. 'This isn't a rush decision, Laura. I've had the last thirty years to think about Exonby, and I made my choices long, long ago. I'm not prepared to discuss them any further. I've already decided what I'm going to do.' He turned away from her again, and picked up the Biro that lay on the desk.

'Then I resign.'

'Don't be childish, Laura.'

'It's not childish! I'm absolutely appalled! You tell me of these plans of yours that are no more than blatant vandalism, wrecking everything your family has built up over four hundred years, and you expect me to carry them out for you? Well, I won't do it!'

'Oh, yes, you will. Even if you resign tomorrow, you'll do just that for the next month. Now I'm going out to discuss the new boundaries with Graham. I'll be back here by lunchtime, and I'll expect you to have made a start on letters to Flowerdew and the auctioneers by then.' He rose from his desk. 'Is that understood?'

'This isn't in the terms of my contract. I didn't come here to do this kind of work.'

'Then rewrite your contract.' The door slammed behind him.

The first thing Laura did was to phone Maltwood House. To her horror, she was told that Sir Anthony had travelled into Cirencester, and would not be back till that evening.

The evening! When Alex had already begun to put his plans into action, and when he planned to fly the following morning! Assuming she did manage to tell Anthony on his return, she would just have time to let Alex know what she had done before he left England. But there would be no time, none at all, for him to absorb the news and reconsider his decisions about Exonby.

She had to believe that he wanted her, that he had been waiting for her to break with Anthony, and was willing to take Anthony's place in her life. But would her ending her engagement be enough to push him into cancelling all these horrifying plans? Would it be enough to persuade him to stay at Exonby?

Now that she had time to think about it, she was not at all sure that it would.

Of course, she had always known that he hadn't originally intended to live at Exonby. But she had hoped—oh, how she had hoped!—that the short time he had spent there had softened his attitudes. She had hoped that he, like her, had begun to dream of a future when the two of them would live together at Exonby Hall. Even a none too calm look at the situation now made it clear to her that this was the most rosy of wishful thinking.

After all, it wasn't the lack of a suitable aristocratic wife that had kept him from Exonby. It was—she knew of a dozen reasons, but to her at that moment it seemed that they all came down to one reason. His family.

Surely, she thought, his inability to come to terms with his split background, his aristocratic father and his working-class mother, was the main reason why Alex had left England in the first place. It was the reason why he had hated Exonby so much as a child. He'd suffered taunts then, as he had done the evening before. If he had stayed he would surely have outgrown his sensitivity to them years before, but he hadn't stayed, hadn't ever stopped running away. And now, if he was ever to live the life she longed for him to live—and to share with her—he was belatedly going to have to come to terms with these old, old hurts.

The night before she had been willing enough to help him to do that. And she was still willing. But it seemed she was going to have to start sooner than she had intended.

She drained her last cup of coffee and went to talk to Lady Exonby, who was resting upstairs, and eagerly waiting to hear about the previous night's dinner. Laura gave her a heavily edited account of it, and made no mention at all of Alex's new instructions. Doggedly, she chattered about local gossip and the state of the gardens while the two of them had a light lunch together.

Then she went to the stables, saddled the mare that she had been riding regularly since she came to Exonby, and set out across the broad acres of the park to look for Alex.

CHAPTER NINE

LAURA found Alex half an hour later, at the far end of Moxon's Wood, striding across a stretch of rough grass with George Graham, the tenant of Home Farm. They both looked round at the sound of her horse approaching. They stood, watching her, until she reached them.

'Hello, George,' Laura said. 'Hello, Alex.'

'Did you want me for something?' Alex asked.

'Actually I did want to talk to you, but it's not urgent. It was such a lovely afternoon that I thought I'd ride out and see if I could find you, but there's no hurry, if you two have business together.'

'Oh, we finished all our business a while ago,' George Graham said with a slow smile. 'It's time I was getting back to the farm, Alex.'

Alex didn't contradict him. George Graham said his goodbyes, strode off towards the path that led through the wood, and they were left alone together.

Laura dismounted. There was a wooden fence twenty yards off, and she led the mare over to this, and fastened the reins around the top rail. Alex stood watching her in silence. Then she retraced her steps to where he was standing.

'There's no point in arguing, Laura,' he said in a harsh voice. 'You won't make me change my mind.'

'I'm not going to argue with you. I'm just going to tell you what I think. And you know what that is, *your lordship*? I think you're running scared.'

The tiniest muscle moved just below his left eye, but apart from that he didn't respond at all.

'You must really have hated coming here when you were a boy, mustn't you?' she went on resolutely. 'Coming to this house where your mother used to be a maid, coming here with your father when your mother wasn't welcome to come back any more, not after she'd messed up our nice, tidy feudal system by marrying above herself. Did they tease you then, Alex Gillon? Did the boys like Anthony rag you because your mother was Maud Higgins from Cirencester? Did they say that it was no wonder you were useless at school, because you weren't really one of them? Because you had all that nasty common blood in you?'

'Stop it, Laura.'

'You ran then, didn't you? You didn't fight back, oh, no, not you. You didn't work hard at school to show them you were just as clever as any of them, you just opted out until you had a chance to run. And then you ran, all the way to New Mexico. You ran and ran. And you know what? You're still running now.'

'Stop it. Stop it, Laura.'

'Oh, no, I'm not stopping it, not until you listen to me! You know what I think? I think that, though you pretend to despise all these lazy aristocrats, really you're just plain scared of them. All the time you're here, you can't help thinking that they're whispering behind your back about your philandering father and the chambermaid he married after he put her in the family way. And you can't stomach that, can you, Alex Gillon? You can't stand firm and ignore what they say, can you? You won't even try to stand firm. All you can think of doing is cutting and running!'

Alex reacted now, rapidly, furiously.

'So what the hell should I do? Stand there and let them drag me down to their level? Try to play their damn games even though I know they'll never let me win? Throw away everything I've earned, in trying to prove I'm really better than them? Damn it, Laura, what the hell else can I do?'

'There are a dozen things you could do with this estate, if only you'd stop running and take a good long look at it!'

'Are there hell!'

'You could invite your mother here, for a start! You could invite your sister here! You could try talking to them, and stop letting stuck-up idiots like Anthony persuade you that you ought to be ashamed of them!'

'And you think they'd come? If you think that, you don't understand the first thing about my family!'

'I understand it a whole lot better than you do!'

'Oh, no, you don't.'

He moved forward, quite suddenly, grabbing her and holding her in a painful grip at arm's length, so that she couldn't escape from his penetrating gaze and the force of his anger.

'All right, *Lady Laura*,' he said through clenched teeth. 'You've told me what you think, so now you can damn well listen to what I think. I think you're worse than any of them. You call them stuck-up idiots, but just you try looking at yourself. You're the one who plays on your title, you're the one who revels in all this washed-out feudalism. You love it all so much you can't face going out and living in the modern world. You can't face building a career and making out for yourself. You're trapped a thousand times more than I ever was.'

'That's not fair,' Laura managed to protest. A thousand alarm bells were ringing in her head. She knew she had taken a risk in attacking him head-on, but it had never occurred to her that he might turn her arguments back on herself!

She set her hands on his outstretched forearms, and tried to pull herself free from his grip, but he was too strong for her, and she couldn't make any impression at all.

'Oh, yes, it is,' Alex growled. 'You know what you're doing, Lady Laura? You're selling yourself. All you think of in life is grabbing yourself a husband and a big house so you can queen it over dinner parties like the rest of them. You don't love Downing. You're selling yourself to him for the sake of his pretty house and his rolling acres.'

'I'm not! Alex, I——'

'Oh, yes, you are! You know very well Downing's wary of me, and you know why? Because he knows that if I wanted to, I could bid higher. And just like the little whore you really are, you'd throw over Downing and Maltwood like a shot if you thought you could get me and Exonby instead. Wouldn't you?'

'Alex!'

'You don't like that, do you? Well, let me tell you something. I don't like it either!'

'But, Alex, you have it all wrong!'

'Do I?'

'Yes!'

His eyes were boring into hers. Her arm was growing numb where he was gripping it with all his strength. For an infinite moment he held her gaze, then, slowly, his grip loosened, and he said in a low, almost defeated voice, 'Then tell me how.'

Laura shook her head, trying desperately to hold on to the threads of her concentration. It mattered so much that she should convince him. Nothing less than the truth would do.

'I'll be honest, Alex,' she said quietly. 'There's some truth in what you say. I did want a rich husband, of course I did. Girls from my sort of family generally do marry rich men like our fathers, it's expected of us. I wouldn't have married without love, though, and I honestly thought that I loved Anthony.'

'Past tense?'

She nodded. 'I—oh, it's so hard to explain. I've never had that much to do with men. I never felt inclined to play around, I wanted to wait until I married. I'd known Anthony for years, and my parents had often said that they hoped we might suit each other. Then in my last year at university I started to see him regularly, and—well, I thought that what I came to feel for him was enough.'

'Enough?'

'As much as I could feel. I knew I wasn't carried away with passion, but I didn't really believe in all that. I'd never felt it, and I didn't think I was the kind of person who could feel it. Anyway, I didn't think it was the right basis for a marriage, I thought it was best to marry someone suitable whom you cared about in a civilised way. And then I met you, and——'

'And you learned about pure, savage lust,' Alex finished for her, with grim amusement.

'I learned a lot, Alex, and I'm still learning. But as you know, I'd already promised to marry Anthony, and I didn't want to rush into breaking my engagement without thinking carefully whether I was doing the right thing. You can understand that, can't you?'

'Yes, I can. And are you sure now?'

'Very sure. It hasn't been easy, because I've seen so little of him over the past few weeks. But I told myself I'd make my decision last night, and now I've made it.'

'So you plan to end the engagement.'

'Yes. I've already tried to tell him, but he won't be back at Maltwood till early this evening. I'll go over there then, and give him back his ring.'

There was a moment's silence. Laura added, more tentatively, 'I'm not taking it for granted that you... I mean, whatever happens, I know now that it wouldn't be right for me to marry Anthony.'

'You know how I feel about you,' Alex said gruffly.

'And I feel the same about you.' She held his eyes, and said, in a quiet but sure voice, 'I love you, Alex.'

'I love you too.' His other arm came round her, and he pulled her close. For a moment he just held her tight against him, then he tipped up her chin with his hand, and bent to claim her lips.

His kiss had nothing of savagery, but plenty of passion in it. It was as if he was freeing, in one glorious cloudburst, all the pent-up feeling of the previous days. His hands brought her body to caress his, gently but insistently. She brought her own arms up to link at the back of his neck, and gave herself to the embrace wholeheartedly.

Both their breaths were ragged by the time he slowly drew his mouth away from hers.

'You'd better go and see Downing,' he said quietly.

'I'll do that now.'

'I'll be here till five or so, then I'm going back to The Chequers. Will you come over there?'

'As soon as I possibly can.'

It was ten o'clock by the time Laura left Maltwood House, after several exhausting hours of argument with Anthony, and tears and recriminations from his mother. Both of them had begged her to take time to reconsider her decision, and Anthony had complained long and loud that Gillon had stolen her from him. She had tried to explain to him that Alex hadn't given her any encouragement, and that the decision was entirely her own, but he had guessed that she would be going to Alex as soon as she left, and she didn't feel able to lie to him.

It would have been pointless to lie, in any case, because he would know soon enough that she was to marry Alex. And she couldn't feel guilt or regret for long, when her heart was so full of the joy of her new-found love.

He did love her, he did! She had won through, and they would be together at Exonby! The miles seemed to fly by as she followed the barely familiar roads that led to the country hotel.

The Chequers had originally been a village pub, but it had been extended several times, so that it now consisted of a square of converted cottages clustered around a pretty, flowered courtyard.

Alex was in the bar, where he had promised to meet her, and one look at her joyful expression told him that she had done as she had said she would.

'Let's go to my room,' he said. He led her across the courtyard, and unlocked the door. 'I ordered some champagne for us here,' he continued, as he moved inside the room.

'Champagne two nights running!'

'Why not? We're celebrating!' He caught her up and whirled her round, narrowly missing the bed and the colour television, before setting her on her feet and kissing her resoundingly.

'To us!'

There was only one chair, so they sat side by side on the bed, laughing and kissing and drinking the champagne. Alex took her hand, and ran his finger over the slight groove that had been caused by Anthony's engagement ring.

'My hand feels so light,' Laura confessed.

'Not for long! I'll buy you a new ring as soon as I land in the States.'

As soon as he landed! She had somehow assumed that he wouldn't be flying off in the morning at all! But that was hardly realistic of her, she realised; his flight was already booked and he doubtless had a great deal to attend to at Northways. Anyway, she was so delighted by this reassurance that marriage was definitely what he had in mind that she couldn't be too disappointed.

'I'll have to tell you what size.'

'You will. Or you can wait, if you'd rather, until you join me there.'

A tiny frown puckered Laura's forehead. 'Join you? But there's no need for that, is there? I mean, you'll be coming back here very soon, surely?'

She expected a quick and immediate reassurance from him. But there wasn't one. Instead there was a sudden and alarming silence.

Alex got up from the bed. He took one pace away from it—all there was room for, in the little hotel room—then turned to face her.

'Why do you say that?'

'Well, because—because I just assumed you would. I mean——'

'No.'

The single word was full of harshness and venom. Laura couldn't understand it. She couldn't understand why Alex should turn from her again, and pace towards the window like a caged lion.

'I'm never coming back, Laura,' he said harshly. 'I told you that.'

A cold flood of apprehension seemed to swamp her. 'I know you did. But I thought——'

'Then you were wrong.' He turned to her again, sharply. She stared at him. The lines on his face seemed drawn deep in the half-light of the lamp. He looked older, tired, as if he had suddenly remembered an over-whelming difficulty that their earlier euphoria hadn't changed in the slightest.

'There's something I can't work out, Laura. I've been trying to figure it out ever since I came to Exonby, and I still don't know the answer.'

'What is it, Alex?' she barely whispered.

'I want to know who it is you see when you look at me. I want to know just who it is you think you love.'

'Think I love! But I do love you, Alex!'

'Do you?'

He let the silence grow for ten seconds or more, then he slowly approached her. He sat down again on the bed, just out of arm's length.

'You say you love me,' he said slowly, 'and I guess you mean it in your way. But who is it that you love, Laura? Is it Alex Gillon, the garageman from New Mexico? Or is it Alexander George, the Fourth Earl of Exonby?'

'I don't understand you, Alex. I love you! You! The man who's here, with me now. You know as well as I do that you're both those people.'

Alex shook his head. 'Let's put it this way, Laura. It's not a matter of a name, that don't mean a damn. But do you love me as I really am, or do you love me as you wish I were? Do you love the man who decided twenty years ago to put Exonby and all it stood for behind him? Or do you love some man you've dreamed up for yourself, a man who never made that decision?'

'But even the firmest decisions sometimes get changed, Alex. I decided to marry Anthony, and I've admitted now that I chose wrong. Can't you even consider that you too might have chosen wrong? That maybe Exonby isn't such a terrible place as you make out?'

'Maybe it ain't. But I'm not changing my mind, Laura. And I don't want you marrying me, thinking I'm going to change it. I don't want you marrying me, imagining you're choosing a life of dinner parties at Exonby, because it ain't going to be like that. If you marry me it has to be because you chose Alex Gillon and New Mexico.'

He meant it. For the first time, it struck home to her that he meant it all. He really would go back to New Mexico. He really would have Exonby Hall demolished, the park turned to farmland and the servants paid off. He really would renounce his title as soon as he possibly could, and go back to being what he had been for the past ten years and more: Alex Gillon, a garageman from New Mexico.

She couldn't look at him. Her hands came up, unconsciously, to nurse her head. It ached. Too much had already happened that day, and now that they were together, and the shadow of Anthony was gone at last, there was still more than she had dreamed of to be unravelled.

Alex reached out and, with infinite gentleness, ran his hand across her shoulder and caressed the back of her neck. He stroked down the shining mass of her hair, then he said, even more quietly, 'I'm never going to be the goddamn Earl of Exonby, Laura. Even for you, honey, I won't do that. Exonby and the title stands for everything I hate. I have my life now, out in New Mexico, I chose it for myself, and I'm not changing it. I tried to tell you that from the start, but I guess you didn't listen. Maybe you couldn't listen.'

'Maybe I couldn't,' she said wearily.

'I ain't saying you were altogether wrong with what you said this afternoon. You're too damn right that I hated my schooldays. I hated my family. I hated my parents with their quarrelling and their divorce. I hated those visits to Lord and Lady Exonby, and I hated the visits to my mother's family in their scruffy little house even more. I couldn't get out from under that soon enough, and as soon as I was old enough to, OK, I ran. But I stopped running when I got to New Mexico. I stayed there, and I built something that I'm proud of out there.'

'So you should be. Any man would be proud of building up a company like Northways. But Exonby isn't all bad, though. There's a lot that's fine about it, honestly, Alex.'

'Maybe there is. Other people see it, and maybe it's just me that can't. It's not that I have anything against Lady Exonby now. I've nothing against my mother and Fenella. I don't want to see them and they don't want to see me, because we've grown too far apart now, and it would only open up the old wounds, but I dare say they're no worse than anybody else. But I have my life now, and I'm keeping to it.'

'I see that now,' Laura whispered.

'So you see, that's all I can offer you. Alex Gillon, successful garage owner with a business that spans three states of the USA, and a hell of an ambition still to do more. There isn't an Alexander George who'll make you the Countess of Exonby. You won't ever swan it over a dinner like yesterday's at Exonby Hall again, because there won't ever be a dinner like yesterday's at Exonby Hall again. If you ever dreamed of that Alex Gillon, then your dream was an illusion, Laura.'

Laura didn't answer. She couldn't answer. It was as if a veil had been ripped away, but the light behind it was too bright, and she couldn't adjust her eyes to see properly. She could see now just how unreal her day-dreams had been. But at the same time she had been aching to hold and love the man who was sitting beside her—and he was real, wasn't he?

Slowly, slowly, she lowered her hands and turned her head to Alex. He met her look full on, but she didn't try to look into his eyes. Instead she looked at the rest of him, intently, urgently, as if she had never really seen him before.

All the Gillon genes were there. Of course they were. The resemblance to the old earl wasn't astonishing, but it was clear to be seen. His light brown eyes, the arrogant jut of his nose and chin, could be echoed in a dozen portraits hanging in Exonby Hall. But this was the man who had broken the tradition, and chosen to stand alone. He couldn't offer her that heritage, because he no longer possessed it. He could only offer her Alex Gillon.

'I'm not offering to meet you halfway,' Alex said quietly. 'If you want marriage you can have it, but you'll be Mrs Gillon, not Lady Exonby. You'll live in New Mexico, not in Gloucestershire. You'll have a good life out there, but you won't have any fake feeling of being special. There won't be anybody calling you "Lady" in that smarmy tone any more. You'll be thousands of miles from your family and friends, and you'll be marrying a man they won't most of them even try to understand, let alone to like. That's me. That's all I can offer.'

'Alex, I . . . I'm so overwhelmed, turned upside-down, I . . .'

'You don't have to say yes this very minute.' He stood up, and paced over to the window that looked out on to the courtyard. 'I'm going back tomorrow. I told you that, I planned it, and I'm keeping to it. I want you to come over too. Not tomorrow, but as soon as you can fix it. Stay with Kent and Susie-Jo, or at the Marbury. Bring your parents over if you like. Get to know New

Mexico better, get to know me better, and then decide if it's what you want.'

'It's not how I ever imagined myself.'

'I can't change that, Laura.'

She didn't answer. He had his back to her, looking out of the window. She stared at it, but it didn't tell her anything. Her mind seemed to have gone blank. To face up to all that he planned to do with the estate, to end her engagement to Anthony, and then to be made this offer of marriage by Alex—in terms that seemed so inevitable now, but that had, all the same, come as a total shock to her—it was all too much.

Slowly, she got to her feet and approached him again. This time he did not move at all. She put her arms around him, and leaned against the broad expanse of his back, settling her head into the hollow between his shoulderblades. Beneath her fingers, she could sense the steady thud of his heartbeat.

They stood there like that for several minutes. Then Laura raised her head, and gently pulled Alex round to face her. He came without protesting. She slid her arms back round him, and hugged him tightly to her. Then she raised her face to his.

'Kiss me, Alex. Please.'

She saw his hesitation in his face, and for a moment she thought he was going to refuse. But he bent his lips to hers, and slowly claimed them.

His kiss at first was tentative—not demanding, not insisting, but cautious, questioning. But her mouth opened eagerly under his. His effect on her was as instantaneous as it had always been. He was familiar and yet exciting, her counterpart, irresistibly male and foreign. She wanted him. This was the sensation she wanted, this warm burgeoning of desire.

His arms tightened round her, and his mouth moved to drop hot kisses on her temples, her earlobe, the taut column of her neck, the curve of her collarbone. Urgently, her hands roamed across his back, pulling him closer, trying to convey to him the desperation of her desire.

'Love me, Alex. Make love to me now.'

Alex seemed not to hear her. There was blind longing in his movements now, in the touch of his mouth, the caress of his hands over the curves of her breasts and buttocks. His thighs, pressed hard against hers, transmitted the depth of his need to her. When he moved to pick her up, her hands came effortlessly round his neck, and she seemed to float into his arms. He covered the few strides to the bed, then he was laying her down on it, and all but falling on top of her.

'Darling.' She was scrabbling at the buttons of his shirt, eager now to feel his flesh against hers. Her body moved under his, wildly, with a wantonness that she had never before sensed in herself. They would be lovers now, and then all the questions would surely disappear, or answer themselves.

But even as she thought this, she sensed a change in him—a withdrawal, faint at first, then gathering force. A prickle of uneasiness stole through the heat of her desire. She fought to hold his eyes again, but they seemed veiled now, and her glance slithered off them.

Slowly, Alex shook his head.

'No, darling. Not now.'

'Alex?' There was a world of uncertainty, desire and confusion wrapped up in that single word.

He moved clumsily, almost like a sleep-walker, as he got off the bed. 'You'd better go,' he said in a harsh voice.

'Alex, what's wrong?'

'Now is wrong, that's what!' He almost spat the words at her. 'Don't you see? You've not decided, you're not committed. Suddenly you want to make love with me because you think it'll make everything all right. But it won't. It won't give you any answers, it can only tell you what you already know.'

It was true, and she knew it. But that knowledge didn't take away the disappointment, the frustration that swamped her body like a tide of bilge-water. 'Alex,' she whispered. It was almost a plea, though she knew even as she said it that there was no prospect of his succumbing to it.

'I want you to think first,' he said. He turned and began to pace around the room. 'I want you to come back to New Mexico. I'm off balance here, it isn't me that you see here. I want you to come there, where my life is, and spend time there with me. Out there you won't get messed up with this stupid business of the earldom. Out there you'll be able to tell if this is what you really want.'

But I want you here! a small voice inside Laura seemed to wail. I don't want to think over all these hard questions, I don't want to change my life, I just want to make love with you now, here, in this room.

She wouldn't have said any of that to him. Slowly, she sat up and swung her feet to the floor.

'I'll phone you when I get back home,' Alex said quietly.

Home. Home being New Mexico, halfway across the world. She nodded wordlessly and slipped on her shoes.

She meant to leave without touching him again, but he stopped her by the door, and set two gentle hands on her shoulders. 'You do understand?' he asked urgently.

'I—I think so.'

'We can make it work, darling. We can. But it can't be here, it has to be out there.' He dropped a deliberately light kiss on her forehead. 'You'd better go.'

CHAPTER TEN

LAURA was in her office at Exonby, poring over the plans for the west wing, when the harsh ring of the telephone cut across her thoughts.

'Laura Mallingham.'

'Good morning, Miss Mallingham. Greg Evans from the *Daily Recorder*. I'm doing a piece on large-scale conversion projects for our architecture supplement, and I'd like to feature Exonby Hall.'

'An editorial piece? But are you in favour of conversions? Will it be...?'

She reached for a pen and pad of paper, and began to take notes. Of course he was welcome to come to Exonby to discuss the project. Illustrations? She had plenty of photos available, but he could bring his own photographer if he preferred. The architects? She would arrange for their representatives to be on hand.

She sighed with satisfaction as she set the phone down. It was the third request that month from the national Press. The first stage of the conversion had already been shortlisted for a prestigious architecture award, and sales of the flats were brisk.

So much had changed in the year that had passed since Alex Gillon had flown back to New Mexico. From the outside Exonby Hall looked much the same, but inside it had been gutted. The contents had been sold, and the conversion had begun as soon as it was certain that Alex would not receive planning permission to demolish it.

Laura no longer worked in the old study. Her new office was adjoining her flat in the east wing, the first section of the Hall to be completed. It had once been the laundry-room, and was stark and functional, though her flat itself retained the elegant sash-windows and wood panelling of the Exonby Hall she had known.

'Marian,' she said, glancing towards her secretary, 'call Smithers and Smithers, please, and see which of these dates John Smithers can make for a Press interview.'

'Of course, Miss Mallingham.'

'I'm going to lunch with Lady Exonby, but I'll be back by two to talk to the couple who've made an offer for number five.'

She slung her navy jacket over her shoulder as she stood up. On the door was a neat bronze plaque: 'Gillon Estates. L Mallingham, Manager.'

By the time she had parked her car, Lady Exonby was framed in the open door of the Dower House.

'Come and see my chrysanthemums before you come in,' she said imperiously.

They walked together round the small garden at the side of the Dower House.

'And how have the sales gone this week?'

'Two definite, and I'm hoping to firm up another one this afternoon.'

'That must be most of the second phase already sold?'

'All but two flats.'

Lady Exonby nodded. 'You know, Laura, I always felt you were a little wasted as my secretary, but I'd never have believed that a year later you'd have a secretary of your own.'

'Nor would I.'

'And I dare say it wasn't what you thought you wanted, my dear, any more than I wanted to see the old house pulled to pieces. But since it had to be done, I'm glad to know it's been done so well.'

And so am I, Laura thought silently, as she followed Lady Exonby down the tracery of narrow paths. I thought I'd be married by now, and the mistress of a country house myself. But the world has changed, and Alex was right when he tried to tell me that there was more to be gained from changing with it, than from clinging to an outdated past.

Lady Exonby paused to cut a bunch of just-blooming chrysanthemums, and then the two of them passed on into the house, where a lunch table was already set, and dishes of salad and cold meat stood waiting.

Lady Exonby didn't speak again until they had filled their plates and were sitting at the table. Then she said briskly, 'I had a letter from Alex yesterday.'

Laura's fork fell from her hand. 'Alex Gillon?' she asked, in an oddly unsteady voice.

'Precisely. Though I must say, I still find it difficult to call him that. A disgraceful business, renouncing the title. Imagine if he has a son one day!'

'What did he say?'

'He asked me not to tell you, but I found that quite ridiculous. It's not as if he could keep it a secret that he's coming back over here.'

'Coming back!'

'You must have assumed that he'd come back some time.'

'Well, one day, maybe, but I hadn't . . .' Laura murmured, flustered. She didn't like to tell Lady Exonby that Alex had gone out of his way to assure her, when he had offered her the job of running Gillon Estates, that he would never, ever be returning to Exonby.

'One day very soon,' Lady Exonby said coolly. 'The second of October, to be exact. He asked me to arrange a hotel room for him, but I'm sure you can get Marian to do that.'

'Of course,' Laura whispered.

Why, why? Laura kept asking, as she drove back to her office. Lady Exonby had seemed to assume that Alex was coming over to admire the conversion and to check how Gillon Estates was being run. That would be understandable, she supposed, but she couldn't help wondering if his return also had something to do with his feelings for her.

But how could it? She had turned him down, hadn't she? And he wasn't the kind of man who would ask her to marry him twice. He had been bitter and angry at her refusal to come out to New Mexico. She knew it had confirmed all his worst beliefs about her snobbery and materialism. He'd believed that she hadn't really loved him, but only that false image she had built up of the Fourth Earl of Exonby.

Was that true? She hadn't been sure then, and she wasn't sure now. It seemed to her now that she had never really seen Alex Gillon clearly. He'd torn her world apart, then flown back to New Mexico before she had recovered. She had tried to explain to him that she felt—as did her parents, and the few friends in whom she had confided—that she needed time to get over the breakup of her engagement, and to come to terms with the criticisms he had made of her—some of which, she admitted now, were only too accurate—before making the trip. But he had refused to give her that time. He hadn't asked her to agree to marry him immediately, but he had insisted that she come over to New Mexico right away. And she had said no.

Even now, she felt that she couldn't have done otherwise. It wouldn't have worked if she had flown straight to New Mexico. She couldn't have come to terms with herself in that alien environment, as she had been able to do at Exonby. She felt a quiet pride in the Laura Mallingham she had now become—so much more confident and outgoing, surer in her judgements, and asking so much more from life than the Laura Mallingham of eighteen months before. All right, there had been a price to pay—and she had found it difficult to come to terms with the fact that losing Alex was part of that price—but she couldn't really regret paying it.

So the woman Alex would meet on the visit would be different in many ways from the Laura he had left behind a year before, and she, in turn, would see him through different eyes. He surely couldn't be hoping to revive their relationship, but, even if he did, so much had changed that it hardly seemed probable that it would work. No, Laura told herself prosaically, that's in the past now. Most likely this is just a sign that he accepts that it's dead beyond hope of revival, and feels that the two of us will now be able to meet and do business in the normal manner.

Even so, he had wanted to keep his coming a secret from her. To surprise her? Or because he thought she might find an excuse to be away from Exonby if he gave her warning?

Well, she certainly wouldn't do that. It wasn't that she particularly wanted to see him again—or that she would admit that she did, when there was no hope of their getting together again!—but simply that she had nothing to fear from their meeting, and no reason to hide from him.

> 'I'll be arriving at Heathrow on flight ZY 124, due to arrive 6 a.m. on Wednesday 2nd October, and staying in England until Friday 16th October. Staying at The Chequers. Arrange a hire car for me to collect at the airport please.
>
> Alex Gillon.'

Laura read over the curt fax message for the umpteenth time, then turned to Marian.

'You've got the hire car receipt? You've got the hotel booking confirmation?'

'Yes, Miss Mallingham.'

'Your car keys? The spare office keys?'

'Yes and yes, Miss Mallingham.'

'Now, what else will you need?'

'Nothing, honestly, Miss Mallingham.'

'Drive carefully, the M4 can be terribly busy.'

'Not at four a.m.,' Marian said with a grin. 'I don't know, Miss Mallingham, it's not like you to worry.'

'You'd worry, if you'd ever met Alex Gillon before.'

'Worry? I'm looking forward to it!' Marian picked up her handbag and clinked her car keys in her hand.

'I'm sorry to make you go so early, but you'll have all the rest of the day off in compensation.'

'That's OK. See you tomorrow.'

Marian waltzed off, looking a great deal cheerier than Laura felt. Laura stood and watched until her secretary's little Mini had disappeared down the Hall drive, then she went to make a cup of coffee.

It was still only just past four a.m. Alex would be arriving at Heathrow in two hours, and Marian would be meeting him and driving him to The Chequers, where his hire car would be waiting for him. Laura had given a great deal of thought to these arrangements. She hadn't thought it right to leave Alex to drive to Gloucestershire alone on top of a transatlantic flight, but she hadn't dared to meet him at the airport herself.

He would probably want to rest a while when he arrived at The Chequers. Would he come into Gillon Estates that day? Probably not, and if he did it wouldn't be for hours, so what was she so nervous about?

Nothing! But still, she couldn't imagine going back to bed. I'll catch up on some filing, she thought. Even my muddled head should be able to cope with that!

Scrunch. Another car braking on the gravel forecourt; another jump from Laura. The hall residents seemed to have a continual stream of visitors and repair men calling that morning.

But this one was—yes, it was a Ford, just like the car she had ordered from the hire car company. She ran to the window to see if it was Alex, if she could catch a glimpse of him, then scolded herself, and marched resolutely back to the filing cabinet. There was still a small sheaf of papers in the in-tray.

She could hear footsteps on the gravel outside, a clunk as somebody opened the main door to the office suite. Then the inner door-handle turned, and she froze, papers in her hand.

He flung the door open with his usual determination, and strode into the room. Then he came to a dead halt and stood there, arrogant and masterful in a dark business suit, surveying the neat desks, computers, filing cabinets—and her.

'Hello, Alex,' she said softly.

His eyes found hers and held them, and she felt her senses reel. She'd thought she remembered everything about him, but her memory had blurred the impact of his sheer magnetism and charisma. Just to be in his presence was like suddenly discovering an extra sense, like suddenly wakening from a long, deadening sleep.

'Hello, Laura,' Alex replied.

They dined together that evening—early, since even Alex had to admit to a touch of jet lag!—at The Chequers.

Laura didn't dare to refer to their last meeting at the hotel, and nor did Alex mention it.

They talked of the conversions over sherry, and discussed some of Laura's plans for Gillon Estates—which she was hoping to develop to convert other properties, once the work on the Hall was completed—over their cream of vegetable soup. Alex questioned her intensively, and to her relief he agreed all her suggestions in outline. 'You've thought it out well,' he told her.

'Thank you, sir.'

'I always thought you were wasted in your old job.'

'That's true,' she agreed. 'It was enjoyable in its way, but it really didn't stretch me.'

'And now you like being stretched.'

'So I do.' She smiled into his eyes. 'You'll have to watch it, or I might start planning a take-over bid under your nose!'

'No need, I'll willingly discuss a reorganisation of the company share structure when you feel you're ready.'

'I'll think it over, and see if I can come up with some proposals.'

'Do that.' He hesitated briefly, then went on, 'You're very committed to Exonby, aren't you?'

'I love the place,' Laura responded. 'I always did. And I'm glad that—well, that I decided to go on working there.'

He didn't reply, and after a while she went on, 'And how's Northways going?'

It was thriving, as he told her at some length. In fact they talked of the two businesses for the remainder of the meal. It was an absorbing, if impersonal conversation, and Laura was sorry when Alex finally told her he'd have to take an early night.

All the more sorry, as she admitted to herself on the drive back to the Hall, because it looked as if Lady

Exonby had been right. Alex seemed to have come with the intention of vetting Gillon Estates' activities just as thoroughly as he had investigated the Hall's accounts a year earlier. And if he had any other motives—no, he didn't, that was obvious.

She told herself that night, and the following day, that they were perfectly capable of carrying on a civilised business relationship without letting their past emotional involvement get in the way. She even began to congratulate herself on handling the situation so well. And if, just now and then, she found her eyes lingering on Alex's hawk-like profile, that was surely something she could keep to herself.

If there was always a slight constraint underlying Laura's business relationship with Alex, Marian, her secretary, didn't share it in the slightest. She treated him with breezy informality from the start, and he treated her similarly. She flirted with him outrageously, and, if Alex didn't precisely flirt back, he didn't discourage her either.

Laura found this increasingly difficult to bear, and by the end of a week she was beginning to feel that she would scream if Marian made eyes at Alex one more time. It hurt even more, though, when Marian looked over at Alex as she came in one morning and said cheerily, 'How's the hangover?'

'Not too bad,' he responded.

The hangover! Had they had a drink, or even dinner, together the previous evening? Alex hadn't asked Laura to eat with him since that first night. Had he been seeing more of Marian outside the office than she had realised? She couldn't bear to know; she couldn't bear not to know either. She tried to suppress her hurt, and worked on in sullen silence till lunchtime. Alex had arranged to eat with George Graham at Home Farm.

'Have fun,' Marian cooed, as he shrugged on his jacket.

'I'll be back at two, Laura,' Alex said, and closed the door behind him.

'Marian.'

'Yes, Miss Mallingham?'

'Don't you think you could treat Mr Gillon just a little more respectfully? After all, he *is* our employer.'

'Alex doesn't mind.'

'Well, I do!' She shut the file she was working on with an unintentional thud, and Marian gave her a curious glance.

'Somebody here has to be nice to him.'

'You can be nice to him without fawning over him all the time!'

'It's better than freezing him off like you do!'

Laura was too angry to reply. Marian airily picked up her handbag and got to her feet. 'All right if I go to lunch now?'

Laura nodded, wordlessly.

When Marian had left Laura's head slumped forward, and her hands came up to nurse it. She suddenly felt very weary, and very lonely.

Freezing him off! Was that really the impression she gave?

Perhaps it was, she thought reluctantly. It frightened her more and more to realise how strong her feelings for Alex still were. She had been terrified of making them clear to him, so it was no wonder she had found it difficult to treat him naturally.

She sat there alone for several minutes. She had some sandwiches in her desk drawer, but she didn't feel hungry. She didn't feel like working. She wasn't expecting any callers or urgent phone calls. She got up, slowly, and went out of the door.

Once outside, she paused. Over towards the west wing, she could hear cement mixers churning and carpenters sawing. Though the east end of the Hall had been completed and relandscaped, there was still building dust in the air. A workman appeared around the near corner of the building, carrying a can of paint and a brush, and whistling to himself.

She turned away from him, and struck out over the gardens.

She didn't know where she was going, only that she had to get away. She needed to think. She didn't want to face Alex again until she had thought everything through.

She walked erratically—through the old kitchen garden, past the high wall of the orchard, and along towards the woodland. The leaves were beginning to fall in Moxon's Wood. She took a wide path that led through it towards the Upper Lodge, crunching them underfoot, but barely noticing them.

Freezing him off. Was that really what she had been doing?

It wasn't what she wanted to do. She realised that now with stark clarity. What a fool she had been to reject him! He was the finest man she had ever met, she loved him in a way that she couldn't imagine ever loving any other man, and she had turned him down because she was such a blind fool that she couldn't separate out the really important things from the trivial ones like a name, or a grand dinner party.

She loved Exonby, but her love for the place couldn't compare with her love for the man who owned it. She loved her job, but it wasn't the only job in the world. And she knew now, clearly and beyond doubt, what she most wanted. She wanted Alex to tell her that his feelings were unchanged, and to ask her once more to marry him and come with him to New Mexico. If he asked her now, she knew that she would say yes, leave Exonby, her family, and her job behind her and go with him.

But how could she expect him to ask her, when she had been freezing him off ever since he arrived?

A cold wind rustled through the trees, and a flurry of leaves fell on to the path. She looked upwards, and saw dark clouds beginning to form above. The forecast that morning had been for rain. She was already a couple of miles from the house. She turned, and began to walk back along the path, her steps faster now and more purposeful.

The rain began when she was at the edge of the park: sudden sheets of it, a real autumn storm. Even if she ran, it would take her a quarter of an hour to get back to the office. She looked around, and saw an abandoned dovecote, just a hundred yards or so from where she stood. A moment's thought—with the rain lashing now, intensely—and she ran full pelt for this.

Once under the narrow archway that led inside, she relaxed; she would be safe here until the storm ended. She had given orders for the dovecote to be cleaned out ready for restoration a few weeks earlier, and, though there was still a musty smell lingering in the perforated bricks, the floor was swept bare. It was cool and restful in the little domed space.

She leaned against the rough brick of the inside wall, and picked up her thoughts.

They brought her a rueful smile. She had thought she knew what love was a year ago, when she had realised that her feelings for Anthony could never match her feelings for Alex. But she had changed in the last year, and so had her feelings. Her love for Alex then had been a pale shadow of her love for him now. She wasn't any more the cautious, conservative girl who had taken an easy option on life. She knew she would be able to love now in a way that that girl could never have loved, that, if he would only give her a chance, her life could be transformed by this consuming passion for the most arrogant, energetic, restless, demanding man she had ever met.

Give her a chance? But why should it be he who did it all? Didn't she know that he was a man who found it difficult to express his emotions? He was at Exonby—wasn't that enough? Couldn't she make a chance for herself?

What have you done, Laura, she chided herself, to try to win him back? Have you smiled, have you laughed, have you worked at charming him? Have you touched him by accident, have you engineered 'unexpected' meetings with him? No, you've done none of that. You've 'freezed him off'. You've sat and watched while Marian seduces him in the way you long to do yourself.

So why not do it? He's not Anthony, he won't be shocked. Wait till this stupid rain stops, go back to the office, find an excuse to send Marian out, and tell him, for heaven's sake, how you feel about him.

Alex, she said to herself, I've been an idiot. Alex, I was stupid to turn you down. Alex, please give me another chance. Alex, I love you.

The more she rehearsed it, she thought ruefully, the harder it was going to be to say.

But why? They were only words, weren't they? What was she afraid of? What would he do? At the very worst he'd turn her down, but that wouldn't lose her anything, because she didn't have him in the first place.

'I love you, Alex Gillon.' She said it out loud, in the quietest of whispers.

What on earth was she whispering for? Nobody was going to hear her standing in a deserted dovecote, least of all Alex Gillon. The little domed space seemed to grow even darker; the storm was surely at its height.

'I love you, Alex Gillon.' She said it loudly this time. And more loudly, so that the words echoed around the brick dome of the little building. 'Alex, I love you.'

'It's taken you a hell of a while to realise that.'

'Not all that long,' she said absently. 'I knew the very minute you walked into my office, I just haven't known how to say it to you.'

'Exactly like that will do fine.'

'Alex, I——'

It struck her, with dreadful suddenness, that it wasn't a disembodied voice in her head she was replying to, but a real live man. Then a dark shape moved away from the archway and into the centre of the dovecote, and she saw that it was indeed Alex—damp, dishevelled, but unmistakably Alex.

'Alex, what are you doing here?'

'I could ask you that. I was caught by the rain on my way back from Home Farm, not that it matters. What matters, I guess, is that I love you too.' He leaned against the wall opposite her, sliding his feet a pace forward and putting his hands in the pockets of his suit trousers.

Laura's throat had gone dry; her head seemed to be floating away. 'That's all right, then,' she said hazily.

'Not entirely. We still have some pretty big problems to face up to. But I've been thinking those over too, and I guess I can see a way forward.'

'What way?'

Alex's voice grew quiet and serious. 'What happened last year made me think hard, Laura. You said some tough things to me, and I know that many of them were true. In some ways I still was running away from Exonby. I hadn't come to terms with my inheritance, I didn't want to even think about it, and all I could think of doing was to get shot of the whole thing as fast as possible. But that was no answer, and I see it now.'

'Exonby's no problem now,' Laura said slowly.

'True, in the sense that what's done is done. Maybe I did the right thing, maybe I didn't, but it's too late to change it now. But it's not too late to set things straight with my family.'

'Your family?'

'That's one reason why I came over here—to see my mother and sister again, and to see if we could bury the hatchet. I had dinner with them yesterday.'

'Alex!'

'I won't say miracles happened,' Alex said, and Laura could have sworn he had reddened in the dim light of the dovecote. 'We'll never want to live in each other's pockets, but at least we're speaking to each other now. I reckon it laid a few ghosts, if nothing else.'

'Alex, that's wonderful.'

'I wanted to see,' Alex went on, 'if I could bring myself to spend more time at Exonby in future. And I guess the answer is that I could. What I thought I might do is to take one of the apartments in the next phase of the conversion. I'd delegate some of the work I do at Northways, and plan to spend maybe half the year here, and half the year there. Then, if it works out, maybe I could bring myself to sell out in New Mexico, and move back to England for good in a year's time or so.'

'You'd move to England!'

'Well,' Alex said bluntly, 'you ain't never going to move to New Mexico, and I can't stand living without you.'

'Alex!'

'Could you ... do you think ...?'

'Oh, my love, I can't stand living without you either!'

Somehow he was moving forward, and she was moving forward, and they were half falling into each other's arms under the dome of the dovecote.

For a moment their joy was too intense for them to do anything more than hold each other in the tightest of embraces. Then Alex slowly lifted his head, and Laura brought her eyes to meet his. And his mouth came down, slowly, slowly, to rest on hers.

There was a vast peace in their kiss, but at the same time there was the most intense of turbulences. They were starved, both of them, for the touch and feel and taste of each other. Laura's hands and mouth roved across the wide expanse of his back, his neck, his chest, in an absorbed exploration that was distracted only by the exquisite feel of his mouth dropping little kisses on her forehead and temples, and his hands cupping and caressing her breasts, and tracing a leisurely path down her spine.

His hands moved lower, and she gasped as he pulled her hips hard against his.

'Alex! Darling, we can't——'

'Can you think of one good reason why not?'

'But . . . but . . .'

'You want this as badly as I do.'

He was unbuttoning her blouse, one-handed, while his other arm continued to hold her to him, tightly, as if he was half afraid she would run away. Gently he pushed aside the lacy cup of her bra, and his mouth bent down to claim the rosy tip of her exposed breast.

Laura gasped, as shoots of sheer pleasure seemed to drive through her body.

'It's quite private. Nobody'll come.'

'The floor . . .'

'We can lie on my jacket.'

He shrugged it off in a single arrogant movement, and spread it out across the hard, newly swept earth. 'Here.'

Laura's legs wouldn't hold her any more. She subsided weakly on to the floor, with Alex half kneeling over her. His arm came round her, and arched her body up to meet his. She brought her own arms around his neck, and drew him down to join her in a long kiss of consuming passion.

She no longer cared about their surroundings. Nothing mattered but Alex. Alex, here at last, in her arms, holding her close, whispering words of love to her, slowly undressing her and kissing each inch as he exposed it. Alex, telling her that he loved her. As she told him, again and again, her shyness forgotten. Alex, I love you. I love you, Alex. Alex, I love you.

His mouth moved lower, lower, depositing little sharp, biting kisses on the soft skin of her abdomen and her upper thighs. His hand took hers, and encouraged her to ease off his trousers, and to find the hard evidence of his arousal.

She had never known anything as strong as this hot, damp, melting, aching sensation. There was no room for doubt, no room for hesitation. His fingers, his mouth, passionate and confident in their caresses, eased her towards a peak of desperate longing. Then he was pressing against her, gentle but insistent, breaking into her, and the longing was somehow being appeased and intensified at the same time.

Higher he took her, higher. Her eyes had closed, her hands grabbed wildly at the smooth skin of his back. The rhythm of it was taking her, carrying her away, urging her higher still. Then it seemed to gather together into a glorious hot explosion of astonishing bliss, and she was floating back to earth, her breathing as ragged as his, her eyes unfocused as she hesitantly opened them.

'Laura,' Alex whispered, in a harsh whisper.

'Alex. I never...'

'I know you never.' He released her gently, and rolled over on to his back on the earth beside her. 'Now I know. I guess we should have waited, but God, I couldn't wait any longer.'

'Nor I,' Laura murmured.

He gave a short, low laugh. 'If you'd known the nights I spent torturing myself, thinking you might go back to Downing, thinking there would surely be someone else.'

'I never wanted anyone else like this.'

He turned to her and gave her a lazy smile. 'I guess so. Still, I reckon I'd better marry you as fast as I can fix it!'

'You had.' But it still hung on Laura's mind that he didn't know the half of it, and she took a deep breath and went on, 'But, darling, we'll never live at Exonby.'

'Never...?'

She gently shook her head. 'It's the most wonderful thing I can imagine, that you should have been willing to come back for me, Alex, but I won't let you do it.'

'But you told me! That first night I was back, you told me how much it mattered to you to be working here, how much you loved it!'

'It did matter. But I didn't mean that I'd really chosen Exonby over you. I wanted to be here as much as anything because it gave me a link with you!'

'But I thought...'

'Then, darling, you thought wrong.' She kissed him once more, lingeringly, then slowly pushed herself up to a sitting position. 'You're not the only one to have done some hard thinking. You told me I was mixed up, Alex, and it was true, I was. It wasn't just Anthony. It was the whole business of working out who I was, and what I wanted from life.

'I think I'd just taken on the role my parents had set out for me without ever thinking what I wanted for myself. A little job, marriage to a nice, kind, dull man—I never thought further than that. Even the fawning flatterers who called me Lady Laura. It wasn't that I enjoyed it, Alex, it was more that I never even noticed it. I took it all for granted.'

'Until I came along.'

'Until you came, and questioned it, all of it, the good bits and the bad. I got so angry at some of your plans. Even now, I sometimes yearn for Exonby as it used to be—as it was that night of the dinner, when we drank champagne together in the Rose Room. It took me a long time to see beyond that destructive urge of yours, and to realise that I really did agree with so much of your attitude. I didn't want to cruise along all my life, living on the past. I too needed to rethink my inheritance. I needed to carve my own path through life, choose my own career, stretch myself more.'

'You've done wonders, Laura.'

'And I'll do wonders in future, I hope—but in New Mexico, not at Exonby! Come to think, I'll need to do wonders to keep up with Susie-Jo Allen!'

'She'll be so pleased, and Kent too.' Alex smiled, as if he was thinking of how it would be when he brought her home with him.

'I'll be so happy to be friends with all the people I met in New Mexico. So you see, Alex, all that's changed. A year ago, I might have been tempted to say yes if you'd pushed me harder, or asked me sooner. But what you were offering me, your life in New Mexico, really would have seemed to me to be a second best to Exonby. You were right. I was only half in love with Alex Gillon, and half in love with that mythical being, Alexander George!'

'And now?'

'Now I'm choosing to be Laura Gillon, and I wouldn't wish for it to be otherwise.'

Alex too sat up, and began to retrieve his scattered clothes, and shake the worst of the dust out of them. 'I'll make you that just as soon as we can fix it,' he said, as he was dressing.

'As soon as we're back in New Mexico.'

To her surprise, he shook his head. 'No, here.'

'Here? At Exonby?'

'That's what you'd like best, isn't it? To have our parents to the wedding, and all your friends? And I'll invite old Lady E, and the rest of my family too.'

'It is,' she quietly agreed. And then she couldn't help smiling. 'So you finally found something you wanted in England!'

'How true,' Alex murmured, pulling her to him yet again. 'I never wanted the rest of my inheritance, but it suits me fine to inherit your love.'

Janet Dailey ®
Americana

Janet Dailey's perennially popular Americana series continues with more exciting states!

Don't miss this romantic tour of America through fifty favorite Harlequin Presents novels, each one set in a different state, and researched by Janet and her husband, Bill.

A journey of a lifetime in one cherished collection.

April titles   **#29 NEW HAMPSHIRE**
Heart of Stone

#30 NEW JERSEY
One of the Boys

Following the success of WITH THIS RING,
Harlequin cordially invites you to enjoy the
romance of the wedding season with

**BARBARA BRETTON
RITA CLAY ESTRADA
SANDRA JAMES
DEBBIE MACOMBER**

A collection of romantic stories that celebrate the joy,
excitement, and mishaps of planning that special day
by these four award-winning Harlequin authors.

**Available in April at your favorite Harlequin
retail outlets.**

ZODIAC WORD SEARCH CONTEST

You can win a year's supply of Harlequin romances ABSOLUTELY FREE! All you have to do is complete the word puzzle below and send it to us so we receive it by April 30, 1992. The first 10 properly completed entries chosen by random draw will win a year's supply of Harlequin romances (four books every month, one from each of four of the series Harlequin publishes—worth over $150.00).

What could be easier?

S	E	C	S	I	P	R	I	A	M	F
I	U	L	C	A	N	C	E	R	L	I
S	A	I	N	I	M	E	G	N	S	R
C	A	P	R	I	C	O	R	N	U	E
S	E	I	R	A	N	G	I	S	I	O
Z	O	D	W	A	T	E	R	B	R	I
O	G	A	H	M	A	T	O	O	A	P
D	R	R	T	O	U	N	I	R	U	R
I	I	B	R	O	R	O	M	G	Q	O
A	V	I	A	N	U	A	N	C	A	C
C	E	L	E	O	S	T	A	R	S	S

PISCES	ARIES	LEO	EARTH
CANCER	GEMINI	VIRGO	STAR
SCORPIO	TAURUS	FIRE	SIGN
AQUARIUS	LIBRA	WATER	MOON
CAPRICORN	SAGITTARIUS	ZODIAC	AIR

Please turn over for entry details

HOW TO ENTER

All the words listed are hidden in the word puzzle grid. You can find them by reading the letters forward, backward, up and down, or diagonally. When you find a word, circle it or put a line through it. Don't forget to fill in your name and address in the space provided, put this page in an envelope, and mail it today to:

Harlequin Word Puzzle Contest
Harlequin Reader Service®
P.O. Box 9071
Buffalo, NY 14269-9071

NEXT MONTH:
LOOK FOR YOUR CHANCE
TO WIN A COLLECTOR'S
EDITION, AM/FM
OLD-TIME RADIO!!!!

NAME _____

ADDRESS _____

_____

CITY _____ STATE _____ ZIP CODE _____

Rules
1. All eligible contest entries must be received by April 30, 1992.
2. Ten (10) winners will be selected from properly completed entries in a random drawing from all entries on or about July 1, 1992. Odds of winning are dependent upon the number of entries received. Winners will be notified by mail. Decisions of the judges are final. Winners consent to the use of their name, photograph or likeness for advertising and publicity in conjunction with this and similar promotions without additional compensation.
3. Winners will receive four (4) Harlequin romance novels (one (1) from each of four of the series that Harlequin publishes) per month for one (1) year, with a total retail value of $150.72.
4. Open to all residents of the U.S., 18 years or older, except employees and families of Torstar Corporation, its affiliates and subsidiaries.

H2MAR2